THE CLIENT BOOK

A CATALOG OF HUNGERS

ISA BREVINE

ISBN:
Paperback : 978-1-967942-11-4
Hardcover: 978-1-967942-12-1
ebook: 978-1-967942-10-7

Book Cover Design and Interior Formatting by 100Covers.

The First Entry

The silence in my apartment is oppressive. It has weight and texture, a quality of polished, cold steel that hums at a frequency just below hearing. It is the perfect intentional absence of noise, a vacuum I have meticulously engineered.

My apartment is a sterile box of air on the forty-second floor, an open layout of polished concrete where a living area bleeds into a kitchen defined only by a severe island of black granite. My bedroom is not a room so much as a theory, an alcove demarcated from the living space by a subtle shift in the flooring from concrete to a tatami-like mat of woven black grass. The bed is a low platform of ebonized wood, the mattress firm, dressed in severe grey linen. There is no headboard to lean against. Over the bed is a thin, weighted blanket, a therapeutic tool for sensory deprivation I have repurposed for the same effect. By the entryway, a narrow console of blackened steel stands against one wall. On its perfect, dustless surface sits a single matte black ceramic bowl, a placeholder for keys that do not exist and mail that never arrives. It is a space designed for a ghost. There is no clutter, no art, and few personal effects. The entire western wall is a sheet of floor to ceiling glass, three panes thick, a silent, immovable barrier.

Outside this glass, the city is a feverish beast, all sirens and distant, wet-sounding arguments and the ceaseless, messy hum of a million lives I have no interest in. Inside, there is only the soft, deliberate click-clack of my keyboard and the low, rhythmic purr of the server rack in my closet. It is the sound of a mechanical heart, a steady and predictable engine that I can service, that I can control. Control. It begins with the control of one's own environment.

The only light is the stark white rectangle of the monitor, carving my face from the darkness. It feels less like illumination and more like a clinical examination, its cold photons landing on my skin without warmth. A chiaroscuro study in blue-white and shadow. I catch my reflection in the black glass and note the severe, clean lines of a black cashmere turtleneck, the taut, satisfying pull of hair scraped back from my face, and the dark, unblinking eyes of a nocturnal predator. This is the uniform of my other life. The life that happens in the silence… after.

On the screen, the words assemble themselves. I am not writing; I am curating. Each entry a rare specimen of human hunger, its frantic, beautiful struggles stilled by the precise placement of the pin in a theoretical spreading board.

They think they are buying my body. What I am actually selling is a finely crafted mirror. This is my collection of the hungers reflected within it.

My fingers pause over the keys. It is a good opening line. Clean. Precise as a scalpel. It establishes the thesis of the collection, as well as the life I have built to house it. A life of perfect, intentional absence of noise, unpredictable variables, messy emotions, and the chaotic static of other people's needs. I close my eyes for a moment, gathering my thoughts within its quiet, fortified walls.

I open my eyes. The reflection on the screen is still there. A ghost. For a moment, I don't recognize her. There is something in the set of her jaw, a vulnerability in the curve of her mouth that belongs to another girl, a girl I buried a long time ago under a headstone of cool, academic theory. A girl who believed in collaboration, in shared discovery, in the intoxicating perfume of intellectual intimacy. A girl who once filled the margins of her books with a passionate, looping script, her thoughts a chaotic and beautiful garden.

Cassandra.

The name is a password to a deleted file, a fault line under the foundation of my fortress.

Just fatigue. A trick of the light. I dismiss it with a force of will that is its own form of control and continue typing. My language is sterile and academic, cataloging their sighs and trembles with the dispassionate clarity of a seismologist recording an earthquake on a distant, uninhabited continent.

A soft weight of living velvet lands on my desk, a stark contrast to the cold, hard-lacquered surface. Klio, my small black cat, blinks slowly at me in a silent demand for attention. The muse of history, reduced to a furry tyrant who wants her dinner. I stroke her head once, the silk of her fur a brief, startling reality against my fingertips. Her purr deepens, a warm, living engine that serves as a counterpoint to the server's sterile hum. She is the only thing in my life that is not curated, the only variable I allow, because her needs are simple, biological imperatives. They can be met and then dismissed.

My gaze drifts from the screen to the object resting on the corner of my desk. The book itself. The physical vessel for my collection. Bound in dark, oil-tanned leather that smells faintly of tannin and smoke by the only man I would call a friend. Our transactions are based on craft, not confession. Its pages are thick, creamy, archival stock, each one possessing a subtle, thirsty tooth. He had asked me what I was writing. I told him it was a history of art. I wasn't lying. The most elegant lies are always constructed from a shard of the truth.

Tonight, I will print and transcribe the twenty-seventh page. Behind it, two hundred and twenty-three pages of yawning blankness remain. A pristine void waiting for a soul. An entire collection waiting to be acquired.

I finish the entry, save the document, inscribe the page, and shut down the machine. The light dies, and the room plunges into absolute darkness.

The silence rushes back in to reclaim its territory. It always does.

CHAPTER 1

The Architect of Innocence

The elevator ascended in a silent, pressurized rush, a vertical launch into a different stratosphere. It was a hermetically sealed capsule, the air tasting of chilled, recycled oxygen and the faint, metallic scent of its own efficiency. A subtle pressure built in my inner ears, a physical marker of the transition from the common world to his. On the ground floor, the lobby had been a study in ostentatious wealth, with marble floors that bled into infinity and a chandelier that dripped diamonds of light. Up here, on the ninety-second floor, there was only the sound of my own breathing, the whisper of silk against my skin, and the soft, digital chime announcing my arrival. The doors slid open directly into the heart of the empire.

His name was Marc, and his penthouse was less a home than it was a declaration of war on gravity. The front door was a formality. The real entrance was this elevator, which deposited visitors like offerings before a two-story wall of glass. Beyond it, the city was a sprawling circuit board of light, a fever dream of a million lesser lives, their frantic energy rendered silent and sterile by the triple-paned, soundproofed glass. The air, conditioned to a perfect sixty-eight degrees, smelled faintly of Killian Black Phantom and the kind of ambition that consumes oxygen. It was a brutalist cathedral, all polished concrete, sharp angles, and voids of empty space. The concrete floors were so highly polished they reflected the lights of the city below, giving the impression of walking on a confined miniature galaxy. I did not just approve; I felt a hollow echo of recognition, a cold kinship with its calculated emptiness. This was a space that understood the power of a deliberate absence, because it was built like a fortress... or a cage.

He was waiting for me by the window, a silhouette against the glittering abyss. Marc was a man whose name appeared in financial journals with the frequency of a verb. He was built like the columns that held up his ceiling; thick, solid, and immovable. Even in a Loro Piana cashmere sweater the color of wet cement and tailored trousers that cost more than my first car, he radiated a kind of tectonic pressure. As he turned, the light caught the silver at his temples and the profound weariness in his eyes. It was the look of a man who owned the world and was exhausted by the upkeep.

"Aura," he said. His voice was a low rumble that reminded me of distant thunder, the sound of something massive shifting far away.

"Marc," I replied, my tone carefully level and pleasant, always a blank canvas. I set my small, unadorned leather satchel on a slab of a coffee table. It was a single piece of black marble, so cold that a faint mist of condensation immediately bloomed on its surface from the ambient humidity of the room. Inside the satchel was the kit for tonight's performance, though I suspected I wouldn't need much of it. The preliminary call had been... specific.

He gestured to a leather Eames chair, the only object in the room that seemed designed for human comfort. "Drink?"

"Water is fine."

He poured it himself from a chilled carafe, the ice making a tinkling percussive sound against the crystal. He moved with a heavy, deliberate grace. His large hands were hands that had likely signed billion-dollar contracts and strangled the life from rival companies; the knuckles were thick, the nails impeccably clean, an image of controlled power. Yet they looked almost clumsy around the delicate glassware. He handed me the glass. Our fingers did not touch.

Rule one: Let the client lead. Let the silence stretch until they are compelled to fill it. It is in the filling of that void that the true request is revealed. I watched him, my senses cataloging the data. The almost imperceptible tremor in his left eyelid. The way his weight settled into the expensive leather of his chair. The microscopic dust motes that danced in the single shaft of light from a recessed fixture, a chaotic system in this otherwise perfect environment of order.

He took a seat opposite me, the vast expanse of the Persian rug a no-man's-land between us. He didn't sip his own drink, a tumbler of amber liquid I assumed was some kind of scotch. He simply held it, staring into its depths as if seeking an oracle.

"I've built things my entire life," he began, his gaze still fixed on the glass. "Skyscrapers. Companies. Portfolios. Structures designed to last, to dominate the skyline. To be… hard." He said the word as if it were a confession.

I said nothing. I simply listened. My greatest tool. I kept my own breathing even and slow, a placid surface against which his agitation could be more clearly observed.

"I want to build something soft," he finally said, looking up at me. The weariness in his eyes was a weight I could almost feel pressing down on the air between us. "I want to build a fort."

I didn't blink. I didn't smile. I gave him a small, professional nod. The request was unusual only in its specifics, not its substance. The hunger was always the same: a desire for escape. A reprieve. A temporary abdication from the life they had so painstakingly constructed. This was a classic regression fantasy, a desire for pre-lapsarian safety. Specimen acquired.

"Of course," I said. "What materials will we be working with?"

For the first time that evening, a flicker of something other than exhaustion crossed his face. It was relief. A deep, shuddering wave of it. He had presented the soft, vulnerable core of his desire, and I had not treated it as a pathology. I had treated it as a blueprint.

He led me to the master bedroom. It was as stark and vast as the living area, dominated by a bed that seemed the size of a small island. The linens, he informed me with an almost shy formality, were eight-hundred-thread-count Egyptian cotton. The pillows were a mix of down and silk.

"Excellent," I said, running a hand over a cool, crisp sheet. The fabric was so fine it had a faint, sibilant whisper against my palm. "Good tensile strength."

He watched, his powerful shoulders slightly hunched, as I began the work of the gentle architect. I was the curator of this construction. I directed him to move the two Eames chairs from the living room, placing them back-to-back. I showed him how to drape the fitted sheet over the top, creating the main roof beam. He followed my instructions with a quiet, solemn focus, his movements careful, almost reverent, as if he were handling sacred artifacts. We were not two strangers, a titan and an escort; we were collaborators in a sacred, childish ritual.

We used the silk pillows to build the walls, creating a precise geometric pattern on the floor. I anchored the corners of the top sheet with heavy art books from his nightstand, a monograph on

Zaha Hadid, a history of the Bauhaus movement. The irony of using texts celebrating rigid, visionary architecture to hold up a temporary shelter of cotton and silk was a perfect, satisfying footnote.

When finished, it was a perfect temporary structure of white cotton and grey silk. A womb of luxury textiles in the heart of a concrete fortress. It was, I had to admit, a rather elegant piece of soft architecture.

"There's one more thing," he said, his voice hushed. He retrieved a small, heavy-duty flashlight from a drawer. He handed it to me, and I noted the almost imperceptible tremor in his fingers.

"Crawl in," I instructed softly.

He got on his hands and knees, this giant of industry, and disappeared into the low opening. I followed, the scent of clean linen and his expensive cologne enveloping me in the small, warm, and suddenly intimate space. Inside, the city lights were gone, the oppressive scale of the apartment reduced to the gentle slope of the sheets above us. The sound of the building's climate control was muffled, replaced by the sound of our own breathing. It was a sensory deprivation chamber of his own design. There was only the darkness and the single, steady beam of the flashlight in my hand.

He curled on his side, his large frame bent to fit the space. He looked like a colossus folded into a jewel box. He did not touch me. He just watched my face, illuminated by the soft glow of the light.

I removed the final component from my satchel. A book. My own copy, worn and soft at the edges, its spine cracked in a dozen familiar places, the pages smelling faintly of vanilla and time. I opened it to the first page.

"If you please," he whispered, his voice thick.

I began to read. "Once when I was six years old I saw a magnificent picture in a book, called True Stories from Nature, about the primeval forest. It was a picture of a boa constrictor in the act of swallowing an animal."

I read on, my voice even and calm, the words of Antoine de Saint-Exupéry filling the small, dark space. I read about Asteroid B-612, about the king with no subjects, about the baobabs and the rose. And as I read, I watched him. I cataloged the slow release of tension from his jaw, the way the deep lines around his eyes seemed to soften and un-crease, the way his breathing deepened, evening out into the slow, rhythmic cadence of sleep. The deep, shuddering breaths of a man relinquishing a weight so immense he'd forgotten he was carrying it.

The hunger wasn't for sex. I concluded it was for a single, uncomplicated moment of safety. To be small again, in a world that demanded he be impossibly large.

When I finished the last page, he was asleep. His face had lost its hard, executive lines in the dim light. He looked younger. He looked, for the first time, peaceful.

I left the flashlight on, pointed at the ceiling, a temporary star in our cotton firmament. I crawled out backwards, as quietly as I had entered. The invoice, already prepared, was on the kitchen counter. The payment, as per our agreement, had been wired to my account four hours ago.

A perfect transaction. Tidy. No messy fluids, no tangled emotions.

I collected my satchel, stowed the book back into its depths, and let myself out, the heavy door clicking shut behind me with the satisfying sound of a bank vault closing. The elevator arrived, and as I descended, I watched the city's lights rise up to meet me, a silent, captured electrical storm. As I crossed the building's plaza, the only nature I registered were the manicured boxwoods in massive granite planters, their foliage clipped into severe, coffin-like rectangles. It was a form of disciplined, joyless green, a landscape that understood its place. I felt the familiar, satisfying hum of a thesis proven. A specimen collected. A perfect entry for the next page of my book.

Smugness is a cold, clean feeling. It feels like control. And control is everything.

CHAPTER 2

The Judge's Submission

If Marc's penthouse was a brutalist monument to the future, Judge Marissa's home was an archive of the past. A four-story brownstone in the West Village, it smelled of vanilla, lemon oil, and the faint scent of settled authority. The air wasn't conditioned to an artificial perfection; it was thick and uncirculated, tasting of the faint metallic tang of old ink and the dry, sweet decay of paper. It held the weight of history, her history. The floors, a dark polished oak, creaked with a learned deference. The walls were lined with books. Thousands of them. Leather-bound legal texts, histories, biographies, their spines a mosaic of gilt and faded color under light the shade of weak tea. It was a fortress built of precedent.

She was waiting for me in her study on the second floor. A mahogany desk the size of a sarcophagus dominated the room. Its surface was a sea of polished, uncluttered wood, holding only a single leather-bound blotter, a heavy crystal inkwell, and a Montblanc fountain pen resting in a silver cradle. It was the desk of a woman who dealt in finality. Marissa was sixty-two, with a mane of iron-grey hair pulled back in a severe but elegant chignon that revealed the strong bones of her face. She wore a silk robe the color of clotted cream, and her face, unadorned by makeup, was a fascinating roadmap of shrewd intelligence and disciplined control. It was a face accustomed to being a mask of impartiality, and tonight, the mask itself seemed weary. Her eyes, the pale grey of a winter sky, missed nothing. They had likely assessed the truth in a thousand testimonies. Now, they were assessing me. She smelled of expensive, unscented soap and nothing else, a deliberate and total absence of perfume that was its own statement of power.

"Aura," she said. Her voice wasn't a rumble like Marc's had been. It was a finely honed instrument, each word delivered with the deliberate weight of a gavel, the acoustics of the book-lined room giving it a dry, resonant timbre.

"Judge Marissa," I replied, placing my satchel on a leather wingback chair. The honorific was part of the script we'd established. The leather of the chair let out a soft sigh as it took the weight, a sound of old, comfortable complaint.

She gestured to the chair opposite her desk. I sat. The leather was cool against my bare legs beneath my simple black silk sheath dress, the cold seeping through the thin material like a localized hypothermia. The desk between us was a courtroom bench, a battlefield, and a border. She did not offer me a drink. The proceedings had already begun.

"Rule one," she said, her voice dropping into a low, almost hypnotic cadence that vibrated in the room's intense quiet. "You will address me as 'Your Honor.' Rule two: You will answer every question I ask. You will not lie, but you may be evasive. The evasion is part of the game. Rule three: You will not touch me until you are given explicit leave to do so. Do you understand the terms?"

"Yes, Your Honor." My own voice was a placid counterpoint, a carefully modulated frequency designed to reflect, not absorb.

The hunger here wasn't for innocence or for the abdication of power. It was for the inversion of it. For a lifetime, she had been the one asking the questions, the one in the robe, the one whose judgment was final. Tonight, she wanted to be the one under scrutiny. She wanted to be the defendant in the courtroom of her own desire. My role was not curator, but prosecutor.

"Let us begin the deposition," she said, her hands folding neatly on the polished wood of the desk. The light from a green-shaded lamp caught the faint blue of the veins beneath the thin, translucent skin of her knuckles. "State your purpose."

I let a beat of silence pass, the first tool of any cross-examination. I could hear the faint, ancient hum of the house's electricity, the sound of my own slow, controlled breathing. "My purpose is to be a mirror, Your Honor. To reflect the truth of the request."

"A clever answer," she conceded, a slight, almost imperceptible smile touching her lips. It did not warm her eyes. "But a mirror is a passive object. Are you an object, Aura?"

"I am a service. The nature of that service is to become what is required."

"And what is required tonight?" The question was a probe seeking a weakness, a scalpel testing the integrity of a suture.

"A verdict," I said.

The air in the room shifted, the pressure changing as if a heavy door had been opened into a vacuum. Her composure, so absolute, fractured for a single, breathtaking second. In the pale grey of her eyes, I saw a flicker of something ancient and hungry. This was what she had paid for. Not for sex explicitly, but for this. For the thrill of being seen, of being stripped bare by a gaze as clinical as her own.

"Remove your dress," she commanded, her voice a low murmur.

I stood, my movements fluid and unhurried. I turned my back to her, a calculated gesture of trust and vulnerability. I registered the sudden change in air currents on my skin, the space behind me now charged with the intensity of her focus. I reached for the zipper and pulled it down slowly, the sound a clean, mechanical dissent in the room's utter quiet, a single rip in the fabric of silence. The black silk pooled at my feet with a soft, liquid hiss. I stood before her in simple, unadorned black lingerie. The air of the study, which had felt merely cool, now felt actively cold, a change in barometric pressure against my skin. I was not presenting a body for pleasure; I was presenting evidence. Exhibit A.

I sat down again. The shock of the cold leather on my skin this time was acute, a jolt to my nervous system that I consciously cataloged and dismissed.

"Let's try again," she said, her gaze sweeping over me with dispassionate intensity, a slow, methodical inventory. "What is the nature of desire?"

"It is the gap between what one is and what one wants," I answered, my voice even. My own cardiac rhythm remained steady, a testament to my control. "It is the engine of narrative."

"And who is the author of tonight's narrative?"

"You are, Your Honor. I am merely the ink."

She leaned forward, the silk of her robe whispering against the desk, a sound like dry leaves skittering across pavement. "Ink can be spilled. It can stain. It can create a truth or a forgery. Which are you?"

"Whichever the story requires."

It was a chess match played with semantics and sensuality. Each question was a move, each answer a counter-move. For every layer of rhetorical defense I presented, she commanded a layer of physical defense be removed. My gloves. My bra. My heels. Each item was placed neatly on the corner of her desk, a growing pile of discarded arguments. The mahogany was cool and dense under my fingertips, its French polish like a sheet of ancient, solidified time.

As I placed my stockings on the corner of her desk, the sheer fabric a dark, weightless cloud, a ghost of a memory, unwelcome and acute, surfaced. Another desk, this one cluttered not with legal texts but with proofs for a monograph on Renaissance patronage. The scent of that office: stale cigarillos, dry sherry, and the heady, dangerous aroma of intellectual intimacy. Professor Amos Hall's office. He had a similar game, one played not with clothing but with footnotes.

"Give me a sentence, Cassie," he would say, his voice a warm, paternal rumble as he leaned back in his worn leather chair. "Just one. The thesis of your new chapter in a single, perfect line."

And I would. I would distill a month of research into a crystalline barb of an idea, and he would smile, a slow, appreciative smile that made me feel like the most brilliant girl in the world.

"Exquisite," he would murmur, scribbling it down on a legal pad. "A perfect specimen of an argument."

The Judge's gaze on my nearly naked body felt less invasive than the memory of his gaze on my naked mind. He was a collector of a different sort. He did not want my body. He wanted the things I built with my brain, and I, young and hungry for his approval, had let him plunder the treasury. The memory was a thin, cold wire tightening in my gut. I pushed it down. I was Aura now. The collection was mine. The curator was in control.

I was the researcher, but so was she. She was studying me, cataloging my responses, my hesitations, the slight flush on my skin under her relentless inquiry. For the first time, I felt a strange and thrilling kinship with a client. She was not a titan exhausted by his power, but a master craftswoman testing the mettle of a worthy opponent. My intellectual fascination was so complete, so consuming, that the nakedness felt incidental, a mere procedural requirement.

Finally, I was bare. The room was cool, and I felt the goosebumps rise on my arms, a fascinating topographical response I observed with detachment. I felt my nipples go pert in the cool air, a purely physiological reaction to the drop in temperature. I sat in the chair, my posture erect, my gaze locked on hers. I had nothing left to remove but the persona itself.

"One final question," she whispered, her voice now thick with an emotion she had held at bay all evening. The professional mask was cracking under the pressure of her own meticulously constructed scene. She rose from her chair and walked around the desk, her movements slow, deliberate. She stopped before me, looking down. The power dynamic had been physically, finally, inverted. She was the one robed, standing; I was the one naked, seated. The tiny muscle that jumped beneath her left eye was the only sign of her agitation. "You have heard the testimony. You have seen the evidence. I stand before you. What is your verdict?"

I held the silence for one final, excruciating beat. I watched the single muscle that twitched beneath her eye, evaluating the only tell in her otherwise perfect mask of control. Her lips were parted slightly, her breathing almost imperceptible. This was not a game. This was a prayer. The hunger was not for submission. It was for absolution. To be judged by an outsider, by a mirror, and to be found… worthy.

I tilted my head back, meeting her gaze. "My verdict, Your Honor," I said, my voice a low, steady instrument calibrated for this exact moment, "is that the court finds you guilty. Of a lifetime of impeccable suffocating control."

A sound escaped her lips, a half-sigh, half-sob. It was, I reflected, the sound of a lock rusted shut for decades finally giving way. The air in the room seemed to rush into the space that sound created.

"And the sentence?" She asked, her voice trembling.

This was the moment of transaction. The culmination of the entire scene.

"The sentence," I said, reaching out and taking the belt of her robe in my hand, my fingers finally making contact with the warm silk, "is release." The fabric was heavier than I expected, with a dry, whispering texture against my skin.

I pulled the knot, and the robe fell open.

The transaction was as clean as the one with the Architect, but its nature was entirely different. It was not about messy fluids; it was about the messy, brilliant, and long-suppressed truth of a woman's desire to be seen for the creature of appetite she was, not just the paragon of justice she was forced to be.

When I left the brownstone an hour later, the payment was already in my account. I walked through the quiet, tree-lined streets, the cool night air a physical balm on my overstimulated skin. The gnarled branches of ancient ginkgo trees, survivors of a dozen city administrations, formed a skeletal canopy overhead, their leaves not yet fallen. A breeze rustled through them, a sound like dry paper turning. Here and there, a wrought-iron fence protected a small square of earth where the last of a season's hostas were dying back with a kind of elegant, papery resignation. The neighborhood held its history with a quiet structural integrity I could appreciate. I didn't feel the smug satisfaction I had felt after leaving Marc's penthouse. I felt something else. Respect.

Back in my apartment, Klio winds herself around my ankles, a silent, furry question. I feed her, then sit at my desk, the white rectangle of the monitor carving me from the darkness once more.

I open the document. I type the title for the second entry.

Specimen B: The Judge's Submission.

I begin to curate the memory, my language sterile and academic. But as I write, I find myself focusing not exclusively on her hunger as I intend, but on the intellectual thrill of the game itself. The satisfying click of a perfectly executed argument. The pleasure of meeting a mind as rigorous as my own.

Marc, the architect, wants to feel small and safe. Marissa, the judge, wants to break the rules. The hungers are different, but the cage is the same. My collection is growing. And for the first time, a sliver of doubt, thin and sharp as a shard of glass, enters my mind: I am the cataloger of cages. What then is the shape of my own?

CHAPTER 3

The Uncanny Valley

There are hungers that are grand and operatic, desires that carve canyons into a person's soul. Then there are hungers that are small, quiet, and pathetic. Those are the dangerous ones. They are the ones that whisper of a rot that is not grand, but common.

Specimen C was a common rot in a ten million dollar shell.

His name was Leo, and his apartment wasn't a monument or an archive; it was an advertisement. Located in a newly erected glass spire that had torn a sterile hole in the sky over the Meatpacking District, the space was a symphony of beige minimalism and aggressive technology. The lights brightened as I entered, a synthesized contralto voice announcing the temperature and air quality with unnerving pleasantness. The floor to ceiling windows overlooking the city were a sheet of intelligent glass; with a soft chime, they tinted five percent darker to compensate for the setting sun. The scent wasn't the arousal of Killian or the comfort of lemon oil; it was the faint, ozonic hum of expensive air purifiers and absolutely nothing else. It was the smell of a void, a deliberate and total sensory deprivation.

Leo was twenty-six, but he looked younger, like a sketch of a man that hadn't been fully rendered. He wore a grey hoodie made of a material so soft it looked liquid and jeans that had been distressed with the precision of a surgeon. His face was all soft angles and the wide, unblinking stare of someone who spends twelve hours a day looking at a screen. He was the boy king of an app that had something to do with monetizing fleeting human emotions. He was worth a billion dollars, and he had the social dexterity of a vending machine.

"Aura," he said, his gaze skittering away from mine to a fixed point on the wall behind me. "The system has verified your entry. Welcome."

"Leo," I replied, my voice pitched to the exact frequency of pleasant, non-threatening warmth. I placed my satchel on a white marble counter that rose from the floor like a geometric ghost. The stone was so cold and featureless it seemed to absorb the sound in the room. "Thank you for having me."

"Drink? The hydration station can dispense water at any pH level you specify. It can also add electrolytes or a vitamin C infusion."

"Still water is fine."

He nodded and spoke to the ceiling. "System, dispense one still water, ambient." A panel slid open with a soft pneumatic sigh, and a glass of water glided out on a chrome tray. He handed it to me. Our fingertips brushed for a nanosecond, and he recoiled as if from a static shock, nearly dropping the glass before I was able to grasp it fully. The water tasted of absolutely nothing, a testament to its expensive purity.

Rule one: Let the client lead. But with Leo, the silence didn't stretch; it buzzed with a low, anxious frequency. It was an awkward, empty silence he was desperate to fill with code. He cleared his throat and looked at a tablet on the counter as if it were a shield.

"Okay," he said, all business. "So, the parameters for tonight's session are loaded into the shared calendar. Did you review the script?"

"I did," I said. The "script" had been a three-page document outlining a meticulously planned evening of simulated domesticity, complete with suggested lines and emotional objectives. It was formatted like a screenplay, complete with stage directions written in a sterile sans-serif font. [AURA expresses disappointment, but with an undercurrent of affection. Her tone should be wounded, not angry.] It was, without question, the most obscene request I had ever received.

"Great. So, we'll begin with the 'Argument' module," he said, looking at his tablet as if it were a pre-flight checklist. "The inciting incident will be my failure to purchase the correct brand of oat milk. Your objective is to express disappointment and frustration, leading to a five-minute period of strained silence before I initiate the 'Apology' subroutine."

I cataloged the hunger as he spoke. It wasn't for innocence or submission. It wasn't for release or absolution. It was for a rehearsal. It was apparent he wanted to practice a relationship with a paid beta tester before attempting the real thing. He wanted to run a simulation on the most complex, unpredictable program of all: human intimacy.

The performance began in the kitchen. I opened the gleaming stainless-steel refrigerator. The handle cold and unforgiving against my palm, the interior light a pale, clinical blue. I feigned a sigh of theatrical frustration. "Leo, I thought we talked about this."

"What?" He looked up from his laptop, his face a mask of practiced confusion that was two degrees shy of convincing.

"The oat milk," I said, holding up the carton. The cardboard felt flimsy in my hand, a cheap prop. "This is the mass market brand. You know I only like the small batch one from Silver Lake."

The words felt alien in my mouth, physically foul, like soap. They were the words of another woman, a woman who cared about oat milk, a woman who used the word "we" without irony. They were Cassie's words, or they could have been. The thought was a splinter under my nail.

"Oh. Right. I… I forgot," he stammered, his performance less convincing than mine.

"You always forget," I said, turning away, the line delivered with a perfect note of wounded patience. I allowed the prescribed five minutes of silence to descend.

I was the curator, the researcher. But this was not a beautiful, strange specimen I was pinning to a board. This felt… cheap. A forgery. The Architect's pillow fort was an honest expression of a deep need. The Judge's interrogation was a brilliant, complex game. This was a soulless imitation. It was a deepfake of a life. Annoyance, a hot, unfamiliar emotion, pricked at the back of my neck, a somatic dissent I could not catalog away.

He executed the "Apology" subroutine with the clumsy sincerity of a hostage reading a script. I, in turn, executed the "Forgiveness" response. Then came the "Movie Night" module.

We sat on his enormous white Mario Bellini sofa, a vast tundra of expensive bouclé fabric that felt like a synthetic cloud against my skin. The television, a screen the size of a gallery wall, played a romantic comedy he had selected, something called "Meet Me at the Fountain." As per the script, twenty minutes in, I was to initiate physical contact by placing my head on his shoulder.

I did so. His body was stiff, unyielding, a ledge of bone and tense muscle beneath his ridiculously soft hoodie. He smelled of a laundry detergent so expensive it had no scent and the faint, metallic tang of nervous sweat. I felt the awkward weight of his arm come around my shoulders. This was the part of the transaction my body was paid for, but for the first time, the mechanics felt foul. In the other encounters, my body was a tool, an object, an instrument. Here, it was meant to be the vessel for a counterfeit affection, and it rebelled. My skin felt… loud. It registered the texture of his sweater, the ambient temperature of the room, and the dead weight of his arm as a series of low-grade insults.

I stared at the screen, at the handsome actor and the beautiful actress falling in love in a flurry of witty banter and convenient misunderstandings. This was the dream he was trying to download. This was the life he wanted to emulate. A life of oat milk and movie nights and uncomplicated connection. A life I had methodically, surgically, cut out of my own.

He shifted, his hand moving from my shoulder to my hair. His fingers were hesitant, stroking the strands with a clinical curiosity, as if trying to memorize a texture he could not understand. He was like a primatologist examining an unfamiliar specimen. I held myself perfectly still, a living doll. My mind, my fortress, began to falter. The intellectual framework failed. There was nothing to analyze here, no grand theory of desire. There was only the deep, pathetic loneliness of the boy beside me and its horrifying reflection in the void I had mistaken for a fortress.

The words of the script felt foul in my mouth, not because they were fake, but because they could have been real. They were the words of the girl I had buried. They were Cassie's words. This cheap, soulless imitation of a life, with its arguments about oat milk and its prescribed movie night cuddles, was the very thing she had once wanted. And I was now performing it for a fee.

"Aura," he whispered, his voice barely a breath against my hair. The script dictated this was his one moment of improvisation. "Is this… is this what it's like?"

What is what like? Love? Comfort? Normalcy? I had no data. I was a researcher in a field I had never personally entered. I had only ever been its ghost.

"Sometimes," I whispered back. The word was not a lie. It was a confession, and it tasted like grave dirt.

He sighed, a sound of such deep, aching need that it cracked the porcelain of my composure. He believed the simulation. And in his belief, he was making it real enough to show me the precise shape of the life I had murdered.

When the movie ended, I extricated myself with a grace that felt like a betrayal. The payment had been in my account since morning. The transaction was by all metrics, clean.

I stepped out of the sterile lobby and into the neighborhood's clamor. The air, thick with the smell of seared steak from a nearby restaurant and the cloying sweetness of a tourist's perfume, felt like an assault. A flock of pigeons, their feathers iridescent with filth, scattered from a pile of trash with a sound like a deck of dirty cards being shuffled. Even the architecture, a jumble of repurposed warehouses and new glass boxes, felt incoherent, a landscape of appetites with no central thesis.

I felt contaminated. Not by him. By her.

Back in my apartment, the silence is different. It is no longer the polished, cold steel of control. It is the vast, humming emptiness of a server that has been wiped clean, the silence of a corrupted file. Klio rubs against my leg, a warm living anchor in the sudden tide of nothing.

I sit at my desk and open the document.

Specimen C: The Uncanny Valley.

I begin to type, my language sterile and academic. I document his awkward gestures, the technical specifications of his apartment, and the precise wording of his script. But the words feel hollow. The smug satisfaction of the researcher is gone. The intellectual thrill of the game has vanished.

All that remains is a sour residue, a greasy film on my skin that no shower can wash away. The Architect erects a fortress of power against the sky. The Judge walls herself inside an archive of precedent. Their confinements are vast, impressive structures. Leo's is small and beige and looks alarmingly like a normal life.

I look at my own reflection on the dark screen. The severe turtleneck, the scraped-back hair, the unblinking eyes. A uniform. A structure of my own design.

The Architect wants to be a child. The Judge wants to be a sinner. Leo, the Tech Bro, just wants a girlfriend. Which I realize with a sudden and nauseating clarity, is a hunger for a different kind of submission. The submission of the self to the collective, the surrender of the strange and specific for the simple and shared.

I close the laptop without finishing the entry. For the first time, the work feels dirty. Not because of the sex, or the kink, or the money. But because for a few scripted hours, I held up a mirror, and the hunger I saw reflected in it looked far too much like my own.

CHAPTER 4

The Alchemist of Scraps

After the soulless domesticity of the Tech Bro's apartment, I cannot remain in my own. The silence feels thin and breakable, contaminated by the memory of a counterfeit life. It is a greasy film on my psyche, an invisible residue I cannot scrub away. I have an animal's instinct to move, to outrun the scent of a threat that is already inside the den. I exit the building and head off in no particular direction. I just need to feel the cool night air on my skin, to feel the city's indifferent current pull me along. I finally glance up as I pass a storefront, the faded gold leaf of the sign catching the glow of a streetlight, and realize my feet have brought me the five blocks to the only person in the city I think of as a friend. The hour is late, so the shop is dark, its windows full of sleeping shadows. I continue without stopping. The performance with Leo has left a sour residue, a taste of a life whose flavor I scrubbed from my palate long ago. A life that belongs to a girl whose name I no longer use.

That girl, Cassie, had once owned things. Not many, but they were hers. A threadbare rust-colored armchair with a sagging seat cushion. A chipped cerulean ceramic mug with a white interior.

And books. A lot of them. They had been her friends, her weapons, her architecture. After the university, after Amos, after the public vivisection of my career and my character, I had to get rid of them. They were artifacts of a failed state, radioactive with a history I needed to bury.

I had boxed them up, my hands moving with a numb, mechanical efficiency. The spines I had known by touch, the soft, worn corners of my favorites, the marginalia I had written in a fever of discovery; all of it became just dead weight. I found him the way you find all the city's secret mechanics, through a faded sign on a narrow, forgotten street. "Arlo French, Bookbinder." I was not there for a binding. I was there for an erasure.

I pushed open the door, a bell chiming a sound of startling gentleness. The air inside was a physical embrace, warm and thick with the trinity of paper, leather, and that sweet, almond scent of binding glue. He was seated at a massive wooden bench, a large man in his fifties with an unkempt greying beard, planing the edge of a book board. He did not look up.

"I'm not buying," he grunted, the plane whispering across the wood in a sound like a long, satisfied sigh.

"I'm not selling," I said, my voice tight. "I want them destroyed."

That got his attention. He set the plane down and looked at me over his spectacles. His eyes were shrewd, missing nothing. He took in the too-expensive coat I had bought when I first arrived in the city to attend university, the hollowed-out look in my eyes, and the banker's box of books clutched in my arms as if it were a bomb.

"Destroyed," he repeated, his voice a low rumble. "These are books, kid. Not state secrets."

"They're evidence," I said, the words tasting like bile. "Of a crime I was accused of and a life I no longer lead. I want them pulped.

Burned. I don't care. I just want them gone." I set the box on his counter with a thud that felt far too final. On top was a slim volume of Petrarch's sonnets, a well-loved paperback with its spine cracked in a dozen familiar places, its cover worn soft with a decade of reading.

He reached a thick, ink-stained finger into the box and hooked the Petrarch. He opened it, his movements surprisingly delicate for a man of his size. He read a passage from my marginalia, my own handwriting a ghost from another world, its loops and slants full of a passionate certainty I no longer possessed.

"'The wound is the source of the song,'" he read aloud, then looked at me. "You wrote that."

A hot wave of shame washed over me, so intense it caused physical nausea. To have my most private, earnest thoughts examined by a stranger felt like a violation worse than any I had yet experienced. "It's derivative."

"It's true," he countered. He closed the book and looked at me, his gaze direct and unnervingly kind. "You look like a woman who's trying to burn down a library because one of the books has a sad ending. That's not a solution. That's a tantrum."

"You don't know anything about it," I snapped, the words sharp with a pain I refused to acknowledge.

"I know what I see," he said, his voice softening. "I see a thousand dollars of perfectly good academic texts. And I see a girl who looks like she's about to shatter into a million pieces." He paused, stroking his beard, his eyes dropping to the open book in his hands, to the flyleaf where a name was written in a familiar, youthful script. "I'll give you two hundred for the lot. But I'm not going to pulp them. I'll find them homes. With students who can't afford them."

I stared at him. A knot of something hot I could not swallow formed in my throat. My carefully constructed composure, a shell of ice I had spent the weeks of attacks perfecting, began to crack under the sudden warmth of his simple, unadorned decency.

"And," he added, his voice dropping lower. "I'll make you a deal. You look like you need a place to put your new story. Whatever it is. You bring me the pages, I'll bind them for you. Cost of materials only. A book for a book."

I should have walked out. I should have taken my box of ghosts and fled. But I was so tired. So tired of fighting, of explaining, of being misunderstood. I looked at his hands, calloused and stained from a lifetime of fixing things.

"Why?" I whispered.

He just shrugged, a small, tectonic movement of his massive shoulders. "Because everyone deserves a place to keep their ghosts," he said. "Even the ones who pretend they aren't haunted."

That was how it started. I left the books. I took his money. And three years later, I came back with the first entry, one about an eccentric, nameless client. I did not tell him my name was Cassie. I did not have to. He had already read it, scrawled on the inside cover of a book about a man whose wound was the source of his song.

A block beyond Arlo's closed storefront, I face a bustling intersection. It is nearing midnight, but this part of the city is wide awake. I need to reassert the borders of my world, to perform a mundane ritual and prove it is still under my command. The twenty-four-hour organic market on the corner is a suitable laboratory.

The automatic doors slide open with a soft whoosh of refrigerated air. The environment assaults my senses. It is a chaotic soup of competing stimuli, an ecosystem of needs I find tedious. The damp, loamy scent of misted kale from the produce section, the sharp, ammoniac tang of aged cheese from the deli, the cloying, yeasty sweetness of organic bakery samples. The lighting is a flat, unforgiving fluorescent glare that renders everything, including the human skin, sallow and clinical. The sound is a low symphony of discordant elements. The high, frantic squeal of a cart's misaligned wheel is a blade of sound against my eardrums. A toddler lets out a piercing shriek that makes the muscles in my back clench. The tinny, percussive beat from a teenager's headphones bleeds into the air, a senseless and invasive rhythm. A woman near the bakery loudly discusses a rash of some kind into her phone, her voice a wet, intimate intrusion. It is a thick, ugly soup of stimuli, a wilderness of casual intimacy, and I am here to chart a neat path through it.

I take a cart. Its metal frame is cool and solid in my hands, the prow of a small ship navigating hostile waters. I push it with a deliberate, steady pace, my movements a counterpoint to the erratic ballet of the other shoppers. I am not here to browse. I am here to acquire.

My first observation is a young woman in expensive Lululemon yoga attire. She holds two different brands of kombucha, a bottle of popular mass market in one hand and a local Brooklyn brand in the other, her brow furrowed in an expression of profound existential indecision. Her hunger is for optimization, for the algorithmic promise of wellness. She believes the correct combination of fermented tea and branded spandex will grant her a longer, more meaningful life. It is a common and tedious pathology.

I move to the produce section. The misting system activates, showering the kale and chard in a fine, theatrical fog. The water beads on the waxy leaves like tiny jewels. This is where I can exercise true control. I select an avocado, my fingers assessing its form before my thumb presses into the pebbled skin, testing the slight give that promises a creamy, pale green interior free of brown blemishes. A perfect specimen. A small, clean victory of predictive analysis. I choose a lemon, noting its unblemished yellow rind and satisfying heft, a data point indicating a high juice content. Each choice is precise, efficient, and a reassertion of my own flawless judgment.

A man in a wrinkled suit speaks loudly into his AirPods, his voice an aggressive instrument. He is negotiating a deal while selecting a pre-packaged kale and quinoa salad. His hunger is for temporal arbitrage, the belief that he can exist in the boardroom and the grocery aisle simultaneously. He is of course failing at both, his attention fractured and diluted. He does not notice when he nearly collides with my cart. I adjust my trajectory by a mere three inches to avoid contact, a silent, elegant correction he remains oblivious to.

Then I turn into the dairy aisle. And I see it.

An entire refrigerated wall of alternative milks, an arsenal of lifestyle choices. Almond, soy, cashew, hemp. And oat. Dozens of brands in a dizzying array of minimalist cartons, each promising a slightly different version of creamy, plant-based perfection. My gaze lands on the one from the script. The mass-market brand, its familiar blue carton a beacon of trendy mediocrity. The one Leo bought by mistake in our simulated life.

The words I spoke to him, the false, theatrical disappointment, feel like a foul residue in my throat. *You know I only like the small-batch one from Silver Lake.* They were Cassie's words, or they could have been, from a life she might have lived. A life of farmers markets and shared Sunday papers. A life I almost had with Amos, before he revealed himself to be a collector of a different, more parasitic sort. He had not just plundered my intellect; he had plundered the small, domestic future we had been sketching together in pencil.

That simple, shared life was the one I was mourning when I carried my books to Arlo's shop. I stare at the carton, this stupid, mundane object, and I feel the carefully constructed wall between the curator and the specimen begin to thin, to become permeable. The annoyance I felt in Leo's apartment returns, a hot, unwelcome spike of data. It is an emotion without a category, messy and useless.

I bypass the entire section with a sharp, decisive turn. My list does not include oat milk. My life does not require it.

I proceed to the checkout. I choose the self-service kiosk. It is a superior system. A clean transaction with a machine. No forced pleasantries, no clumsy bagging, no unpredictable human error. I scan each item, the crisp beep of the device a satisfying confirmation of each choice, and I pay with a tap of my phone. The small vibration of the completed transaction, a satisfying confirmation of each choice. A perfect, sterile sequence. Yet the contamination remains, a low-grade fever I cannot seem to break.

I exit the building and head back towards my apartment, the cool night air doing nothing to cleanse me of the ghost of a life I never wanted, until the moment I realized it had been stolen from me.

Back in my apartment, the silence remains thin and breakable. I walk past the empty console table, the black bowl a perfect, mocking zero. In the kitchen alcove, the severe island of black granite feels less like a statement of control and more like a tombstone for a life I have never lived. For the first time, I notice the way the recessed lighting casts no shadows, creating a flat, clinical landscape where nothing can hide, and nothing can live. I go to the window and stare out, but the glittering city stares back in accusation, its million messy lives a vibrant, chaotic truth my own sterile box is designed to deny.

CHAPTER 5

The Anatomic Canvas

The gallery after dark was a tomb of beautiful, silent things. The air was cool and tasted of conditioned, recycled oxygen and the faint, mineral scent of plaster dust from a newly installed exhibition. It was a calculated and profound quiet, a space scrubbed of all human messiness, where the only acceptable sounds were the soft, reverent whispers of appreciation and the silent hum of the climate control system. I felt an immediate kinship with the room. It understood the power of a deliberate absence. It was a fortress built of white walls and perfect lighting, and tonight, I was its sole and absolute monarch.

My four-inch narrow black heels clicked with the sharp, definitive rapport of a judge's gavel on the polished concrete floor. Each step was an echo, a percussive announcement of my authority in the vast, high-ceilinged space. The only light came from the track lighting, a series of focused, clinical pools that illuminated each individual piece of art, leaving the rest of the gallery in a landscape of deep, cool shadows. On the walls, massive canvases of abstract expressionism hung like captured storms, all violent slashes of color and chaotic energy, their frantic, beautiful struggles stilled by the perfect placement of a frame. I approved.

In a far corner, isolated by a wide cordon of empty floor, sat a single, magnificent white orchid in a square glass vase. Its petals were a waxy, perfect white, its bloom a masterpiece of biological engineering, its beauty utterly captive to the room's controlled climate. It was a living thing treated as a sculpture. It was a sentiment I understood completely.

He was waiting for me in the center of the main exhibition hall. Simon. In the world outside these walls, he was a man whose name was a currency, a titan of the art market who could make or break a career with a single, dismissive wave of his hand. He wore a dark tailored suit that whispered of obscene expense and a life of aesthetic authority. But here, in the stark, curated emptiness of his own domain, he was just another specimen. His hunger, I had already cataloged from our brief, encrypted correspondence, was a particularly elegant one. It was not a simple desire for pain or humiliation. It was a hunger for sensation itself. He wanted to be stripped of his intellect, his critical eye, his power of judgment, and be reduced to a canvas, a pure surface for the reception of somatic data. He wanted to be a work of art, and I was the artist he had commissioned to create him.

"Aura," he said. His voice, usually a confident baritone accustomed to commanding auction rooms, was a quiet, almost reverent murmur.

"Simon." I did not offer a smile. I walked a slow, deliberate circle around him, my own form of appraisal. I was not looking at the man. I was assessing the material. He stood perfectly still, his hands clasped behind his back, a posture of formal surrender. I could see the faint, frantic pulse at the base of his throat, a tiny, trapped insect beating against the cage of his skin. I could smell the faint, clean scent of his expensive soap and the sharper, metallic tang of his anxiety. The data was clear. He was ready.

"The terms of the commission are understood?" I asked, my voice a cool, level instrument in the acoustically perfect room.

"They are," he confirmed. "The fee has been transferred. My trust is absolute."

"Good." I placed my leather satchel on a severe granite bench. The stone was cold and smooth, its surface a perfect, featureless plane. "Then let us review the contract. Rule one: you will not speak unless spoken to. Your opinions, your analysis, your thoughts, are irrelevant to the process. You are here to feel, not to think. Is that understood?"

"Yes." The word was a puff of surrendered air.

"Rule two: your safe word is 'Red.' If you use it, the performance will cease immediately and without judgment. If you require a brief pause, a moment to recalibrate, the word is 'Yellow.' I may or may not grant it. That will be my choice. Is that understood?"

"Yes."

"Rule three: everything that happens in this room is for my pleasure. Your pleasure is incidental, a byproduct of my process. Your function is to be a beautiful, responsive canvas. Nothing more. Do you consent to these terms?"

"I consent."

The negotiation was complete. The consent, freely and enthusiastically given, was a clean, solid foundation upon which I could build the evening's architecture. "Then the artist is ready to prepare her materials," I said. "Undress."

He obeyed with a quiet, almost solemn efficiency. The expensive suit jacket came off, folded with a precision that was the last vestige of his daytime self. The shirt, the trousers, the briefs. Each item was a layer of his public power being shed, discarded on the cold concrete floor until he stood before me, naked and pale in the focused gallery light. His body was well maintained, the body of a man who understood the value of aesthetics, but the muscles in his thighs and abdomen were quivering with a fine, almost invisible vibration of anticipation. He was no longer a collector. He was the un-framed, un-curated, raw material.

In the corner of the room, an object leaned against the wall. A St. Andrew's Cross, crafted from the same dark, polished steel as the frames of the paintings. It was a beautiful brutalist piece of furniture. "Assume the position," I commanded.

He walked to the cross and placed his back against it, his arms and legs spread in the classic X of submission. I retrieved four lengths of soft black leather and four sturdy leather cuffs from my satchel. I bound his wrists first, the leather cuffs cool and smelling faintly of tannin against his skin. I pulled the straps tight, securing his hands to the upper arms of the cross, the metal cool and unyielding beneath his palms. Then his ankles. He was now fixed, exposed, a living sculpture presented for my consideration.

I stood before him, my own clothes a stark black uniform against his pale, vulnerable flesh. I ran a hand over his chest, my fingers tracing the line of his sternum, the hard cage of his ribs. His skin was cool, the goosebumps that rose in the wake of my touch a fascinating topographical response. His heart was a frantic drum against my palm. He was a perfectly primed instrument, waiting for the first note.

I began with a flogger, its suede falls a soft, heavy weight in my hand. The first strike was gentle, a test. The tails landed across his stomach with a soft, percussive thud, a sound that was immediately swallowed by the vastness of the room. He flinched, a sharp intake of breath his only response. I increased the rhythm, the force. The sound became a steady, hypnotic beat, the thud of leather on flesh a primal drum against the gallery's civilized quiet. I was not just hitting him. I was painting with sensation. Broad strokes across his chest, his belly, his thighs. I watched the color rise on his skin, a delicate pink flush that bloomed under the impact, a beautiful, temporary blush on the pale canvas. His head fell back, his throat exposed, a low groan finally escaping his lips as the steady, rhythmic contact overloaded his senses, to short-circuit the analytical part of his brain.

When his skin was a warm, uniform pink, a perfect underpainting, I switched implements. I chose a single tail whip; its leather thin and flexible, a calligrapher's brush for a different kind of art. "The details now," I murmured, more to myself than to him.

The first lash was a line of fire. It landed on his right pectoral with a sharp crack that echoed like a gunshot. A thin red line, a welt, bloomed instantly on his skin, a shocking slash of crimson against the delicate pink. He cried out, a sharp, involuntary sound of pain and pleasure. I delivered another, a mirror image on his left pectoral. Then another, bisecting the first, creating a crosshatch of sensation. I was not a sadist. I was a pointillist. I worked with precision, creating a pattern of fine, stinging lines across his torso, each one a sharp, distinct data point in the overwhelming flood of sensation I was creating. His hips began to move, a slow, unconscious grind against the unyielding steel, his body seeking a release he was not yet permitted to have. His cock, which had been semi-hard, was now fully, painfully erect, a deep, bruised purple in the clinical light.

I set the whip aside. The canvas was prepared. Now, for the final layer. I retrieved two thick, black candles from my satchel, their wax a low-temperature blend designed for this specific purpose. I lit them, the hiss of the match a tiny, violent sound, the two flames two small, dancing stars in the cool darkness. The air filled with the faint, clean scent of burning wax.

I stood before him, a lit candle in each hand. "The final glaze," I said, my voice a low hum. I tilted the first candle, and a single, perfect drop of hot black wax fell onto the center of his chest.

He screamed, a raw, ragged sound of shock that was part of the art. The wax was not hot enough to burn, but the thermal shock was a brutal, exquisite violation. The drop hit his heated skin and immediately solidified, a small, black, glossy jewel against the red and pink of his flesh. I let another drop fall. And another. I was a painter again, dripping a new medium onto my work. The drops were random at first, a chaotic constellation on his torso. Then I began to form a pattern, a slow, deliberate line of black wax from his navel down to the base of his straining cock. He was sobbing now, quiet, desperate sounds, his head thrashing from side to side, his mind completely gone, his body just a collection of nerve endings firing in the dark.

I set the candles down and approached him. His skin was hot, slick with a fine sheen of sweat, decorated with the beautiful, temporary trauma I had inflicted. I took his cock in my hand. It was rigid, burning hot, the veins standing out in sharp relief. A single, clear bead of pre-cum glistened at the tip, a perfect, crystalline tear. I leaned in, my mouth close to his ear, my breath a warm cloud against his skin. "You wanted to be a work of art," I whispered. "And now you are. A masterpiece of sensation. And now, the artist will sign her name."

My tongue darted out and licked a stripe of sweat from his neck. He tasted of salt and fear and a profound, bottomless need. My hand began to stroke him, my rhythm slow and merciless. He was close, his hips bucking, his breath coming in ragged, desperate gasps. He was begging for it. But the release was my decision, not his.

I retrieved the final tool from my satchel. A sleek black vibrator, its surface a cool, non-porous silicone. I switched it on; the low, powerful buzz an alien, mechanical sound in the room. I pressed the head of it against the base of his shaft, the vibrations a deep, seismic shock that traveled through his entire body. He screamed again, a sound of pure, helpless overload. I moved the vibrator to his perineum, the buzzing a relentless, targeted assault on his most sensitive nerves, while my hand continued its steady, rhythmic work on his shaft.

"Look at my work," I commanded, my voice cutting through his haze of sensation. His eyes, which had been squeezed shut, fluttered open. He looked down at his own body, at the beautiful, brutal tapestry I had created. The pink flush, the red welts, the black jewels of wax. And he came.

It was not a gentle release. It was an explosion. A full-body convulsion that seemed to tear through him, his back arching, his throat raw from a scream that had no sound. His orgasm was a desperate, violent, and utterly beautiful surrender. A final messy splash of white on the canvas.

The transaction was complete.

I turned off the vibrator. The sudden silence was deafening. He slumped against his bonds, his body limp, his breathing a series of long, shuddering sighs. I worked in reverse, my movements efficient. I peeled the solidified wax from his skin, each piece coming away with a soft, satisfying pop, leaving a pale, unmarked patch of skin behind. The evidence of my work was temporary, a memory written on the nervous system, not the flesh. I unbuckled the leather restraints, and he slid to the floor, a boneless, beautiful ruin at the foot of the cross.

I dressed in the quiet, the black silk of my Tom Ford dress a cool, familiar comfort. He did not move. I approached the granite bench where my satchel sat and carefully stowed the tools I had removed from it previously. He was still in the place I had sent him, a quiet, thoughtless landscape of pure feeling. A perfect transaction. Tidy. No messy fluids on my person, no tangled emotions.

I collected my things and walked to the door, my heels clicking a final, definitive rhythm on the concrete. I did not look back. I did not need to. I had created a masterpiece, and like any good artist, I knew when the work was finished.

As I walked out into the cool night air, the city's indifferent hum a welcome and familiar song, I felt the satisfying calm of a thesis proven. I had taken a man of intellect and power and, through the careful application of sensation, had reduced him to a pure, responsive instrument. I had proven once again that the body is just an engine. A beautiful, predictable machine that I could service, that I could control.

Control. It was a cold, clean feeling. It felt like coming home.

CHAPTER 6

The Stillness of the Frame

The first thing I noticed was the smell. It wasn't the aggressive statement of a cologne or the sterile hum of an air purifier. It was the smell of work. A layered ancient scent of turpentine, linseed oil, and the sharp metallic tang of photographic fixer that pricked at the back of my throat. Underneath these chemical top notes was the dusty, organic base of old wood, oxidizing canvas, and the profound, settled quiet of a space where time was not measured in minutes, but in the slow curing of paint. It was the smell of captured things.

Julio's studio was a cavern carved out of the top floor of a pre-war warehouse in Tribeca. The ceilings were twenty feet high, ribbed with old timber beams from which a fine, almost invisible dust perpetually fell. A wall of north-facing windows stood grey and opaque with grime, taming the afternoon light, sifting it into a diffuse, milky softness that felt less like illumination and more like a clinical anesthetic. Canvases in various states of completion were stacked against the walls like fallen tombstones, their surfaces turned inward, guarding their secrets. The floorboards, wide planks of scarred pine, creaked with a learned deference under my heels.

The only modern thing in the room was the camera. It sat on a heavy tripod in the center of the space, a black, complex machine with a lens like a single, unblinking, obsidian eye.

He didn't greet me at the door. He was already standing by the camera, a man who seemed to have been assembled from shadows and sharp angles. Julio was famous in a way that required no last name. His portraits were brutal, hyper-realistic things that seemed to flay the soul of his subjects, pinning their most vulnerable truths to the canvas. He was perhaps fifty, gaunt, with a shock of silver hair and eyes that didn't just look, but assessed with a kind of gravitational pull, drawing all light and information into them. He wore a paint-splattered black shirt and jeans. He was the antithesis of my other clients; he had no polish to shed, only layers of profound, unnerving focus.

"Aura," he said. It wasn't a greeting. It was a confirmation of a label, a data point verified.

"Julio."

He gestured with his chin toward a faded velvet fainting couch, its fabric worn to a soft patina in the places where bodies had once rested. "The light is right. Please undress."

There was no preamble, no offer of a drink, no stretching silence to be filled. The transaction was absolute. I was here to be an object, and he was here to be the artist. It was, I told myself, the purest version of my work. The thesis made manifest. I felt a familiar, cool confidence settle over me as I began the process of disengaging the corporeal self. This was a language I understood.

I placed my satchel on the floor and undressed with an unhurried, deliberate grace, my movements a familiar, calming ritual. The air was cool against my skin, raising goosebumps I consciously ignored, cataloging them as a simple physiological response to the ambient temperature. I was not a woman feeling a chill; I was a form preparing for observation, a specimen being prepared for the slide. When I was naked, I looked at him, awaiting instruction. His gaze was not lecherous or even appreciative. It was the gaze of a master carpenter examining a piece of wood for its grain, its flaws, and its potential.

"On the couch," he said. "Recline. Left leg drawn up slightly. Right arm draped over your head. Turn your face toward the window, but keep your eyes on the lens."

I moved, my body falling into the pose. It was a classical odalisque, a pose of languid, available beauty. My mind, my fortress, immediately began to file references. Ingres's Grande Odalisque, with its impossible spine. Manet's Olympia, with her confrontational, commercial gaze. I was placing myself within a historical framework, an act of intellectual control. I knew the lines. I knew the history of the female form as a landscape for the male gaze. I was the curator, and this was my field. I could perform this role perfectly.

He didn't speak again. He moved behind the camera, disappearing behind its mechanical authority. The silence in the room deepened, broken only by the faint hum of the city outside, the whisper of his movements on the dusty floor, and the sound of a lone fly buzzing near the high windows. Then came the first sound.

Click.

The shutter was a quiet metallic blink, a sound of surgical precision. A moment of my existence, stolen and stored.

He adjusted a setting on the complex body of the camera, the dial making a soft, ratcheting noise. *Click.*

He moved a large white reflector board a few inches to the left, the scrape of its stand against the pine floor a brief, sharp retort in the quiet. *Click.*

My job was stillness. Absolute, intentional stillness. My breath was shallow, a controlled and minimal exchange of gases. My muscles locked into the pose. I was a tableau vivant. A living picture. At first, it was easy. My mind, my fortress, was cataloging the scene. The dust motes dancing in the shafts of light were a chaotic system I could analyze. The precise geometry of the shadows under the couch was a study in negative space. I was analyzing the composition, critiquing his use of chiaroscuro. I was safe inside my head, the curator of my own objectification.

Click.

An hour passed. My muscles began their rebellion. It started not as a burn, but as a low, insistent signal from the body's betrayed provinces. The deltoid in my raised arm began to transmit a message of deep, aching fatigue. My hip flexor screamed in a silent, taut line of protest. The stillness was no longer a performance; it was a physical demand. The silence was no longer professional; it was oppressive, a heavy blanket smothering my thoughts. His focus was a physical weight on my skin. He would emerge from behind the camera, his eyes narrowed, and adjust my hand by a millimeter, his touch cold, brief, and utterly impersonal, as if he were adjusting the limb of a mannequin. Then, he would retreat into the darkness behind the lens.

Click.

Another hour. The sun shifted, and the light in the room turned from silver to a pale buttery gold. He adjusted the aperture to compensate; the mechanism's whirring a soft, predatory sound. My mind began to fray. The intellectual framework, my shield, was failing under a sustained somatic assault. I was no longer thinking about Ingres. I was thinking about the cramp building in my calf. I was thinking about a phantom itch on my nose that I could not scratch. I was thinking about the insistent, maddening ache in my shoulder socket. I was thinking about the fact that I had become nothing more than a collection of lines and shadows for the machine in front of me, a machine that did not tire.

Click.

He was the curator now. I was the specimen pinned to the velvet board of the fainting couch.

My gaze, fixed on the lens, began to see a mirror instead of a machine. A round, black, perfect mirror reflecting a world in miniature. And in it, I saw a distorted reflection of my own face. A face of curated emptiness, the severe, clean lines of the persona I had built. The perfect "Aura" persona. A beautiful blank. An image without a soul, with a profound vacancy in the eyes.

The thought was a physical blow now rather than an analysis. The smug satisfaction I felt with the Architect, the intellectual thrill I felt with the Judge, the annoyance I felt with the Tech Bro; they were all gone. All that remained was a profound, terrifying chill that had nothing to do with the temperature of the room. It was the cold of the void. This right here was the ultimate expression of the life I had built. To be perfectly controlled, perfectly observed, and to feel absolutely nothing. To be a perfect object. A beautiful dead thing.

Click.

The sound made me flinch. It was not a decision. It was a violent neurological dissent, an involuntary tremor that ran through my thigh in a brief, spastic shudder. A mutiny of the flesh.

"We're done," he said immediately, his voice flat. The spell was broken.

He didn't look at me again. He was already fiddling with the back of the camera, his attention transferred from the subject to the artifact. The payment had been wired that morning. The transaction was complete.

I unfolded my body from the couch, my joints stiff and protesting, a series of small, painful reports from the front lines of the rebellion. I dressed quickly, my hands clumsy, my fingers feeling thick and unfamiliar. The simple black turtleneck felt less like a uniform and more like a shroud, its soft cashmere an abrasive insult against my overstimulated skin. I picked up my satchel and walked to the door without a word.

"The prints will be ready in a week," he said to my back. "I'll send a courier."

I paused with my hand on the doorknob. I didn't want the prints. I didn't want a record of my own hollowness. But I simply nodded and left, the heavy door closing behind me with a final, definitive thud.

I walk, my head down, the city is a blur of hostile motion. The faces of passersby are a gallery of grotesques, their mouths open in unheard conversations. The only thing I fully register is the stubborn Ailanthus trees, the so-called "trees of heaven", growing from a crack in the pavement by a subway grate. They are a tenacious, ugly form of life that refuses to be curated or killed, their leaves giving off a faint, foul smell like burnt peanut butter as I pass.

The cold clings to me all the way downtown, a chill that has settled deep in my bones. I don't go home. I walk instead, to a narrow, cluttered street in the West Village, to a shop with a faded gold leaf sign that reads: "Arlo French, Bookbinder."

The bell above the door chimes, a familiar, gentle sound. The warm, humid embrace of the shop's air is an immediate, welcome shock. It smells of the usual; old paper, leather, and the sweet, almond scent of binding glue. It is the smell of stories, of things being made whole.

Arlo is at his workbench, a mountain of a man with a wild grey beard and hands stained with a half a century of ink. He is the only man I call a friend. He looks up over his spectacles.

"Cassie," he grunts. It is a statement, not a question. He is the only person who uses my real name. "You look like you've seen a ghost."

"Just cold," I say, running my hands up and down my arms, trying to rub away the phantom sensation of the pose.

"It's sixty-five degrees out," he says, not missing a beat. He gestures with a bone folder to a stack of pristine, cream-colored pages on his desk. "Your paper came in. Archival stock. Last you a thousand years."

I walk over and pick up a sheet. It is heavy, with a subtle texture. Perfect. I am still Aura, the curator, discussing the materials for her collection.

"The binding?" I ask, my voice still tight.

"Oil-tanned leather, as requested. Blind debossing on the cover. Simple. Elegant." He leans back, his stool groaning in protest, and crosses his thick arms. His eyes, shrewd and kind, settle on me. "Brought me any new pages today?"

"I finished an entry this morning. I'll print it tonight."

He nods slowly, stroking his beard. "Right. Another one for the collection. The Architect. The Judge. Who was it today? The Candlestick Maker?"

"A photographer," I say, my voice flat.

"Ah." He looks at the perfect, empty sheet of paper in my hand. "So tell me, kid. All these stories you're collecting. All these people.

It's beautiful work. The writing is clean. Precise. But it's cold. Colder than you are right now."

He leans forward, his voice dropping. He isn't my bookbinder anymore. He is my friend.

"I've got just one question, Cassie," he says, his gaze holding mine, refusing to let me retreat into the fortress. "Where are you in all this?"

I open my mouth to give him the standard answer. That I am the observer. The researcher. The curator. But the words won't come. All I can see is my own empty face reflected in that black lens. All I can hear is the finality of the shutter.

Click.

I have no answer for him.

The Vivisection

The seduction was not about the body. Not at first. The body was an afterthought, a pleasant and convenient postscript to the scintillating text of the mind. The true consummation, the one that left me breathless and undone, happened in the cluttered, sun-drenched sanctuary of Professor Amos Hall's office.

It was a room that smelled of intellectual divinity: the sweet, nutty aroma of dry sherry, the almost-cloying vanilla of aging paper, and the sharp, masculine tang of the Swisher Sweets he perpetually chewed but never lit. It was a scent I would forever associate with being truly seen. For five years, the graduate program at the university had been a blood sport, a relentless gauntlet of scholarly combat where ideas were weapons and egos were casualties. But in Amos's office, the war ceased. Here, I was not just another hungry doctoral candidate. I was his brilliant girl.

"The mistake everyone makes with Bronzino," he would say, leaning back in his great, groaning leather chair, a rumpled bear of a man with eyes that held the accumulated light of a thousand libraries, "is that they see the surface. They see the cold, enamel perfection of the paint and they assume it is a portrait of emotional sterility."

I, curled in the worn armchair opposite him, a glass of sherry warming my hand, would lean forward, the scent of the room filling my lungs like an intoxicant. "But it's not sterility," I would counter, my own mind catching fire from his spark. "It's armor. The silks are not just fabric; they are a form of polished steel. The jewels are not adornment; they are fortifications. He is not painting people. He is painting the beautiful, suffocating architecture of their power."

Amos would listen, his head tilted, a slow, appreciative smile spreading across his face. It was a smile that felt like a benediction, a holy thing that bypassed all my defenses and went straight to my core. It was a smile that said, *I see you. I see the magnificent, complex machinery of your mind, and it is beautiful.*

"The architecture of their power," he would murmur, scribbling the phrase onto a yellow legal pad with a fountain pen that scratched with a sound like a tiny, satisfied sigh. "Exquisite, Cassie. A perfect distillation."

He was a collector of my thoughts. I would bring him the raw ore of my research, the half-formed ideas I wrestled with in the lonely hours of the library stacks, and he would hold them up to the light, turning them over and over, showing me the facets I had not yet seen. I gave him these ideas freely, joyfully. They were offerings laid at the altar of his approval. The intimacy was heady, more potent than any physical touch. It was a meeting of minds so profound, so complete, that when his hand first brushed mine as he refilled my sherry glass, the physical contact felt less like a beginning and more like a continuation, a logical and inevitable extension of the conversation we were already having.

The first time he kissed me, it was in the hushed and holy silence of the rare book room, the air thick with the scent of vellum and time. He had been showing me a first edition of Vasari's *Lives,* and his fingers, tracing the embossed leather of the cover, had found mine. He had tasted of sherry and secrets, and the kiss was not a predator's lunge, but a scholar's discovery. It was a confirmation of a thesis we had both been quietly writing for months.

Our affair was a secret, but it did not feel sordid. It felt sacred. It was an extension of the office, of the library, of the work. It was in the tangled sheets of his bed, in the quiet, post-coital darkness, that my most brilliant ideas were born. They were whispered into the hollow of his shoulder, confessions of intellectual passion that he would greet with a low groan of appreciation, his hand stroking my hair.

"The wound as the source of the song," I had whispered to him one night, after we had spent hours debating the brutal, unseen violence in late Renaissance portraiture. "They are all portraits of beautiful, bleeding things. The painter is not just an artist. He is a seismologist, recording the tremors of a soul under immense pressure."

"My brilliant, brilliant girl," he had breathed into my hair, and I had felt a sense of belonging so profound it was a physical ache. He did not just want my body. He wanted the things I built with my brain. And I, young and incandescent with love and ambition, had given him the keys to the entire treasury. I had let him plunder it, believing it was an act of collaboration, an act of love. I had not yet learned that some collectors do not wish to co-own. They wish to acquire.

The discovery was a quiet, mundane event. A vivisection performed under the flat, unforgiving fluorescent lights of the campus bookshop. It was my sanctuary, a place of holy quiet where the ghosts on the pages were friendly. I was browsing the "New Arrivals" table, a ritual of procrastination, my fingers trailing over the glossy covers.

And then I saw it.

It was a handsome, academic volume, its cover a stark, serious navy blue. The title, *The Gaze as Governance: Power and Patronage in Medici Florence*, was a familiar country. But it was the name beneath it, embossed in a self-important gold serif font, that made the air in my lungs turn to ice.

Professor Amos Hall.

My hands, I noted with a strange, clinical detachment that was the first tremor of Aura's birth, were perfectly steady as I picked it up. The glossy dust jacket was cool and smooth, a liar's skin. My heart was a cold, terrified bird beating futilely against the cage of my ribs. I opened it to the table of contents. My breath stopped.

The chapter titles were not echoes. They were my children, dressed in another man's clothes.

Chapter Three: *The Armor of Venus: Bronzino and the Material Culture of Defense.* My phrase. *The architecture of their power.*

Chapter Five: *Vasari's Coded Gaze: Portraiture as Political Obedience.* The subject of a feverish, sherry-fueled debate that had lasted until three in the morning.

Chapter Seven: *The Wound as the Song: The Unseen Violence in the Late Renaissance Subject.* My whisper in the dark. My most private, most precious, most vulnerable thought, laid bare for the world.

The shock was not a hot, emotional wave. It was a cold, clean, scientific event. It was the moment the world, which had been fluid and full of light, solidified into a block of ice around my heart. I did not need to cross-reference. I did not need to check my notes. I was a mother who knew the precise shape of her child's face.

The theft was not just of ideas. It was an autopsy of the soul. He had reached into the most intimate spaces of my mind, my work, my love, and had harvested the best parts for himself, leaving the rest to bleed out on the linoleum floor of a university bookstore. He had not just stolen my words. He had stolen the late nights, the moments of discovery, the private language of our intellectual and physical affair, and he had presented it to the world as his own solitary genius.

I bought the book, my voice a stranger's as I spoke to the woman at the counter. I carried it back to my carrel in the library, a small, beige cell where I had been slowly, painstakingly building my life's work. I did not cry. Crying was a luxury I could not afford. The grief was too vast; the rage too pure. It was a white-hot hum in my veins, a terrible, clarifying energy. I put the book on my desk next to the bound copy of my dissertation proposal. A case file. Evidence of a crime. I still believed, in my naivete, that evidence was enough. I picked up the book and walked to his office. I was no longer a student. I was a prosecutor, and I was going to war.

The office door was ajar. The familiar scent of it reached me before I even stepped inside: stale Swisher Sweets, dry sherry, and the heady, dangerous perfume of intellectual validation. It was the smell of my own undoing.

He was at his desk, a great, rumpled bear of a man, marking a student's paper with a red pen. He looked up as I entered, and his face broke into that familiar, paternal smile, a smile that had once made me feel like the most brilliant girl in the world. A smile that now looked like the baring of a predator's teeth.

"Cassie, my dear," he said, his voice the warm, familiar rumble that had once felt like home. "To what do I owe the pleasure?"

I did not return the smile. I walked to his desk and placed the book between us. The navy blue cover was a judgment on the scarred and cluttered landscape of his desk.

"A question, Amos," I said. My voice was preternaturally calm, a thin sheet of ice over a raging sea. "Chapter seven. The core thesis. The wound as the source of the song. Where did you get it?"

He looked down at the book. He did not look surprised. He looked weary. He took off his glasses and rubbed the bridge of his nose with a theatrical sigh. It was a gesture I had seen a hundred times, the gesture of a great mind burdened by the smallness of the world.

"Ah," he said. He looked back up at me, the smile gone, replaced by a mask of weary disappointment. It was the look he gave undergraduates who had failed to grasp a basic concept. It was a look designed to make me feel small. "All scholarship is a conversation, Cassandra. A dialectic. We build on the ideas of others. You and I, we have had so many wonderful conversations over the years. This book is the culmination of those conversations."

"This was not a conversation," I said, my voice shaking now, the cold control beginning to fracture. "This was a monologue. My monologue. That chapter is lifted, in places verbatim, from my dissertation proposal. My footnotes are your primary sources. You took the half-formed ideas I shared with you in confidence, the sentences we spoke in bed, and you published them under your name."

He sighed again, the sound of a patient man dealing with a hysterical child. "You are a brilliant girl, Cassie. Truly. One of the best I have ever had. But you are emotional. You are seeing conspiracy where there is only collaboration. A mentor's role is to shape a student's raw material. You gave me those ideas. Freely. As a student. As... a friend."

The word friend was a scalpel. It slid between my ribs and severed something vital.

"I was your lover," I said, the words tasting like poison and shame. "And I was your research assistant. I trusted you. And you have committed the most profound and cowardly theft I can imagine."

His face hardened then. The paternal warmth vanished, replaced by something cold and hard and ancient. It was the look of a king whose divine right had been questioned by a peasant. The look of an institution protecting itself.

"Be very careful what you say next," he said, his voice dropping to a low, dangerous whisper that was more frightening than any shout. "You are a graduate student with a reputation for being… intense. A bit of a zealot. I am a tenured professor, the head of this department, with a sterling forty-year career. Who do you think the board of review will believe?"

I looked at him, at this man I had adored, this man who had been my intellectual sun, moon, and stars. And I saw him for what he was. A vampire. A forger. A man who had built his beautiful, celebrated career on the bones of other people's brilliance. Mine was likely not the first skeleton in his closet. He had not only stolen my work. He had stolen my voice, and he was now threatening to steal my sanity. He was showing me, with a chilling lack of sentiment, that the cage was much larger and much older than I had ever imagined.

The hearing was held in a small, airless boardroom on the third floor of the administration building. The room smelled of industrial carpet cleaner and quiet desperation. The long, polished mahogany table felt like a coffin. I sat on one side, a stack of my meticulously organized evidence before me: my dissertation proposal, dated research notes, early email correspondence with Amos where I had outlined the very ideas that now appeared in his book. I was a scholar. I believed in the sanctity of evidence.

On the other side of the table sat the board of review. Three men and one woman, all of whom looked at me with varying degrees of pity, suspicion, and boredom. They were not my peers. They were my executioners. Amos was not present. He was the plaintiff, the victim of my "unfounded and defamatory allegations."

The chairman, a man with a soft, pink face and the dead eyes of a bureaucrat, began. His questions were not about textual analysis or the provenance of an idea. They were about me.

"Miss Williams," he said, his voice a soft, polite weapon. "Can you please describe for the committee the nature of your relationship with Professor Hall outside of the academic context?"

The air left my lungs. "We were… involved. Personally."

"Involved," he repeated, the word dripping with a salacious distaste. "For how long were you involved, Miss Williams?"

"Two years."

"And during this two-year period, did you consider the work you were doing for him, the 'conversations' you had, to be part of your formal duties as a research assistant, or part of the… personal aspect of your relationship?"

The trap was so elegant, so perfectly constructed, it was almost beautiful. If I said it was professional, they would ask why I had not documented my contributions more formally. If I said it was personal, they would dismiss my claims as the bitter, revisionist history of a woman scorned.

"It was both," I said, my voice small.

The woman on the committee, a history professor from a different department whom I had once admired, gave me a look of thin, weary sympathy. "Cassandra," she said, her voice laced with a condescending kindness that was worse than their contempt. "Relationships between students and their mentors are… complicated.

Feelings get hurt. Perceptions become skewed. Is it not possible that in your emotional distress following the end of your affair, you have perhaps… exaggerated your intellectual contribution?"

Emotional distress. Skewed perceptions. Hysterical. The words were the bars of the cage, snapping shut around me. I looked at their faces. They were not seeing a scholar who had been plagiarized. They were seeing a graduate student who had slept with her professor and was now making a scene. The narrative was simple, brutal, and as old as the institution itself. I was not a victim. I was a liability.

I felt myself begin to dissociate, a survival mechanism kicking in. I was no longer in my body. I was floating near the ceiling, looking down at the specimen in the chair. A young woman in a grey dress, her face pale and her hands clenched in her lap. I watched them dismantle her, piece by piece, with their polite, murderous questions. I watched them take my brilliance, my passion, my work, and re-brand it as the obsessive, vindictive fixation of a jilted lover. The vivisection was now a public spectacle. They were not just killing my career. They were killing me.

The verdict arrived a week later in a thin, sterile envelope. The formal, institutional language was a masterpiece of ass-covering. "After a thorough review, the committee finds no conclusive evidence of academic misconduct." It was over. He had won. He had not just stolen my past. He had stolen my future. There was no place for me here anymore. I was a ghost in a machine that had already moved on.

That was the day Cassandra Williams died. She died in her small, beige carrel, surrounded by the ghosts of her own best words. The first act of my new, unnamed life was one of demolition. The books had to go. They were not simply objects; they were artifacts of a failed state, the sacred texts of a religion I no longer believed in. I packed them into banker's boxes, my hands moving with a numb, mechanical efficiency. The spines I had known by touch, the marginalia I had written in a fever of discovery, and the smell of their pages. It all became just deadweight. Evidence.

I sold them to a gruff, kind bookbinder in the Village who saw the shattering in my eyes and offered to build me a new book, a place to keep my new story. I took his money. And I walked out into the city, a ghost myself, with a blueprint for a new life taking shape in the ruins of the old one.

A life of perfect intentional absence. A life of control. A life where I would no longer be the specimen on display for all to study. I would be the curator. I would be the one holding the pen.

I needed a new name. A name that was a shield. A name that was a surface. A name that meant nothing and everything. I thought of the cold, untouchable beauty of Bronzino's subjects, of the shimmering, immaterial quality of their power. I thought of the almost holy light that surrounded them. Their aura.

I would call myself Aura. And I would be magnificent. I would be hollow. And I would be... a mirror.

The library, once my sanctuary, became my laboratory. My research skills, honed over years of chasing footnotes through dusty archives, were repurposed. I traded texts on Renaissance patronage for treatises on clinical psychology, biographies of famous courtesans, and bootlegged manuals on rope bondage and sensory deprivation. I studied the semiotics of desire not as a theoretical exercise, but as a practical curriculum. I learned the language of power exchange with the same dispassionate intensity I had once applied to Vasari's prose. The internet provided the granular details: the forums where men confessed their hungers in anonymous, desperate detail; the encrypted websites where services like mine were priced and cataloged. I cross-referenced their desires, building a taxonomy of human need.

I was not just creating a persona; I was completing a new doctorate in a field of my own invention. My body became my final, unwritten chapter, and I rehearsed its performance in the mirror until the reflection was a stranger I knew with absolute intimacy. I was no longer a scholar. I was the architect of a flawless, beautiful lie, and my own skin was the blueprint.

But a blueprint is not a building. The first transaction was a clumsy, terrifying affair. He was a mid-level finance drone I found through a discreet online listing, a man whose hunger was for a simple, unimaginative dominance he lacked in his own life. I met him in a sterile hotel room that smelled of industrial carpet cleaner and my own fear. My performance was stilted, a collection of theories I had not yet learned how to inhabit. My voice, which I intended to be a cool instrument of control, had a slight, humiliating tremor. I remember focusing on the texture of the cheap hotel bedspread, a rough polyester landscape, to anchor myself outside the theater of my own clumsy, fumbling body.

He was satisfied, but I was not. The transaction was messy. Inelegant. I had not been a mirror; I had been a nervous amateur. I returned to my apartment that night not with a feeling of power, but with the cold, clarifying shame of a researcher whose first experiment has failed. That failure became my new thesis. I did not just need a new name; I needed an entire methodology. I refined the process. I established the rules that would become my armor:

the encrypted communications, the upfront wire transfers that sanitized the exchange, the deliberate cultivation of a reputation for intellectualism and detachment that would attract a better class of specimen. I learned that the greatest power was not in the performance of sex, but in the curation of the silence that surrounded it. I failed, and failed again, until the performance was no longer a performance. It was a second skin.

It was a cage so perfectly constructed; I forgot I was the one who had built it.

CHAPTER 8

The Violinist's Hands

Craig's duplex, a 1940s gem overlooking the park, was the first client space that felt truly inhabited. It wasn't a declaration of war on gravity like Marc's, nor a fortress of precedent like Marissa's. It was a resonant chamber. The air smelled of old wood, rosin, and black tea. The walls were a controlled chaos of framed sheet music, and the afternoon light, thick with dust motes, fell across the worn spines of a thousand books on composition and theory. It was the den of a man who didn't just live with his art; he was slowly being consumed by it.

He was younger than I'd expected. Thirty-five, perhaps, with a nervous energy that seemed to vibrate just under his skin. He had the lean, ascetic build of a marathon runner and a storm of dark hair that he constantly pushed back from his brow. But his power, his entire net worth, was concentrated in his hands. They were beautiful anatomical marvels of long, elegant fingers and prominent knuckles. They were hands that could coax miracles from four strings of gut and wood. As he made tea, I watched them move, cataloging the precise, economical grace. They were the source of his genius. They were also; I was about to learn, his cage.

"Thank you for coming, Aura," he said, his voice soft, almost apologetic. He didn't look at me directly, his gaze fixed on the steam rising from the porcelain cups. "The terms are as we discussed?"

"They are," I said, placing my satchel on a worn Chesterfield sofa.

He nodded, taking a deep, shuddering breath. This was the moment I always watched for—the relinquishing of the public self. The air in the room thickened with the weight of the unsaid. He gestured to the center of the living room, where a single armless chair stood waiting.

"Please," he whispered.

The hunger wasn't for pain or for power. It was for silence. He lived in a world of constant sound, from the music in his head, the endless hours of practice, to the roar of the adoring crowd. What he wanted was the utter abdication of his own talent. To be helpless. To create nothing.

His hands, those instruments of divine precision, were suddenly clumsy. The buttons of his linen shirt seemed to present an unsolvable puzzle, his long fingers fumbling with the small discs of pearl. He finally pulled it free, letting it fall to the floor. He slid his trousers and briefs down his lean legs, stepping out of them as if shedding a skin he had worn for too long. He stood before me for a moment, not posed or presented, but simply bare. The body was no longer the famous musician; it was just a man, pale and unadorned in the afternoon light, stripped of his art, his name, his defense. He walked the final few feet and sat in the chair, his posture straight, his gaze fixed on a point just past my shoulder.

The kit for this was simple. Four lengths of dark red velvet rope. I worked with the quiet efficiency of a surgeon preparing her instruments. He sat in the chair, his posture rigid, his eyes closed. I started with his right hand, securing his wrist at his side, tied neatly to the outer spindle of the chair back. The velvet was soft against his skin. My touch was clinical and firm. I bound his left wrist to the other side. Then his ankles to the legs of the chair. He was secure. He was still. The celebrated hands, insured by Lloyd's of London for eight figures, were rendered utterly useless.

He let out a slow sigh. The deep, shuddering breath of a man setting down a weight. The same sound I'd heard from the Architect. The cages were different, but the sound of release was universal.

"Now," he said, his voice strained. "In the corner. The case."

I turned. It was leaning against a bookshelf, a modern, carbon-fiber case that looked incongruous in the old-world room. I carried it back and laid it at his feet.

"The combination is 1741," he said. The year the violin was made.

The latches clicked open. I lifted the lid. There, nestled in a bed of crushed blue velvet, was the Vieuxtemps Guarneri. I wasn't an expert in violins, but I was an expert in objects of devotion. I knew its history. I knew what it was worth. More than the penthouse. More than the brownstone. It was a near-priceless artifact that was also a living thing. It seemed to hum in the room's quiet, its dark amber varnish glowing in the fading light.

"Please," he said, his eyes still closed. "Play for me."

This was the core of the transaction. He didn't want me to touch him. He wanted me to touch his soul.

I lifted the instrument. It was shockingly light, a delicate bird's skeleton in my hands. The bow was a perfectly balanced extension of my own arm. I was a curator, a researcher. I could analyze the object, discuss its provenance, its role in the history of music. But I could not play. This was not part of the script.

"I don't know how," I said, my voice flat. It was a simple statement of fact.

A single tear traced a path from the corner of his closed eye down his temple. "It doesn't matter," he breathed. "Just… make a sound. Any sound. A sound that is not mine."

I hesitated. Then, I lifted the bow, drew it across the strings.

The sound that emerged was a screech. A raw, ugly, amateurish noise that scraped the serene silence of the room to shreds. It was the sound of a cat being strangled. I flinched, expecting him to cry out, to end the session.

Instead, he smiled. A genuine, beatific smile of pure release. "Again," he whispered.

So I did. I dragged the bow across the strings again, and then again. I produced a cacophony of ugly, artless noise. And with every tortured scrape, I felt the tension in his body release further. He was a high priest of beauty, and I was performing a desecration on his altar. And it was setting him free. I was proving to him that his instrument, without his hands, was just a wooden box. His genius was the gilded prison, and for a few minutes, I was letting him hear the silence outside the bars.

But then, something shifted. My fingers, resting on the neck of the violin, found a position by accident. My arm, drawing the bow, fell into a rhythm. A single, clear note emerged. It wasn't a screech. It was pure, resonant, and heartbreakingly beautiful. It hung in the air between us, perfect and unexpected.

Craig's eyes snapped open. They were wide, fixed on me. He wasn't looking at Aura, the blank canvas. He was looking at the source of the note.

My analytical mind, my fortress, tried to reassert control. *This is an anomaly. A random confluence of pressure and position.* But my body wasn't listening. I drew the bow again, and another clear note followed. Then another. I wasn't playing a song. I was just discovering the sounds, one by one. The academic fell away. The curator dissolved.

I was no longer a researcher observing a specimen. I was a conduit. The instrument in my hands was alive, and it was teaching me its language. All the longing, the discipline, the frustrated genius of the man tied to the chair seemed to flow up through the floor, into my body, and out through the strings. The ugly sounds gave way to a strange, melancholic melody I didn't recognize and couldn't possibly have known.

The room filled with the music. It was a raw, untutored sound, full of passion and mistakes, a sound no Juilliard-trained master would ever dare to make. It was the sound of a soul improvising. I looked at Craig. His head was thrown back, his face a mask of agony and ecstasy. A taut line of muscle stood out on his neck, and his hips strained forward. His erection pulsed and throbbed, a dancer to the tortured rhythm I was playing. Tears were streaming down his face now, silent and unchecked. He was listening to his own heart being played by a stranger's hands.

The notes grew faster, more complex. My fingers flew, my arm burned. I was lost in it completely and utterly. There was no client, no transaction, no book. There was only the music, the vibration of the wood against my chin, and the impossible, beautiful sound filling the space. It was his hunger, his genius, his pain, and for a few breathtaking minutes, it was also mine.

As the melody reached its frantic, almost unbearable crescendo, his body answered. A low groan was torn from his throat, a human counterpoint to the violin's cry. His whole body went rigid, a final, shuddering chord held for a breathtaking instant, and then he slumped in his bonds, spent. His release was a silent offering on the altar of the sound, a final, messy, desperate note of his own. I ended on a high, soaring note that hung in the air until it faded into nothing.

The silence that followed was different. It wasn't empty. It was vibrating.

I stood there, breathing heavily, my heart pounding. The bow hung limply in my hand. I had no memory of the melody I had just played. The researcher, returning to the lab after a blackout, found all her notes were missing.

I placed the violin carefully back in its velvet womb and closed the lid. I walked over to Craig and, with steady hands, untied the velvet ropes. He didn't move. He just sat there, his head bowed, his beautiful hands resting, palms up, on his knees. The faint, sharp scent of his release mingled with the rosin and old wood. They looked quiet. Peaceful.

I collected my satchel. The payment had been wired. The transaction was complete. I let myself out without a word.

Back in my apartment, Klio purrs, a low rhythmic engine in the quiet. I sit at my desk; the monitor carving my face from the darkness. I open the document, my fingers poised over the keys.

Specimen E: The Violinist's Hands

I begin to type, my language sterile, academic. I write about the objectification of talent. I write about the psychology of release. But the words feel like lies. They are the field notes of a researcher who has, for the first time, become part of the experiment.

I close my laptop. The silence rushes in. But it isn't the cold, polished steel I am used to. It is resonant. It still holds the ghost of a note. And for the first time, I am not entirely sure it is a sound I can curate.

CHAPTER 9

The Collector and
The Question

The transaction before Arthur was a palate cleanser. A reminder of the baseline. Specimen F: The Collector. His name was irrelevant. His hunger was for the purely aesthetic, but unlike Julio the photographer, his medium was not light; it was flesh.

He'd booked a suite at the Baccarat, a place so saturated with crystal it felt like living inside a diamond. The air was chilled and heavy, scrubbed of all organic scent and replaced with the clean, mineral fragrance of white flowers and immense wealth. Light did not simply illuminate the room; it fractured, refracting through a thousand faceted surfaces, casting prismatic, jittery rainbows on the pale grey walls. It was a beautiful, static vivarium, and I was the prize specimen about to be placed inside. He was a man in his forties with the soft, manicured hands of someone who has never had to open his own door and the cold, appreciative eyes of a jeweler examining a stone for its clarity and cut. He wanted, in his words, "a living sculpture."

The performance was simple. I was to lie on the bed, naked, while he appreciated me. I was not to speak. I was not to move unless he moved me. The bed itself was a vast landscape of white, the sheets a high thread count percale that felt cool and unnervingly smooth, like a sheet of polished marble against my skin.

He began with my feet, his touch reverent and impersonal. He traced the line of my arches with his thumb, the slight drag of a callus I had not expected the only flaw in his otherwise seamless presentation. His gaze was analytical. "Perfect," he murmured, more to himself than to me, the word a clinical assessment, not a compliment. He worked his way up my body with the slow, methodical pace of an art appraiser, his touch a uniform pressure, as if testing the provenance of a piece of porcelain. My calves, the curve of my hip, the plane of my stomach. His hands were warm; his touch firm. I cataloged the sensations with my usual detachment. This was a study in surfaces. The slight rasp of his thumb against my flesh. The pressure of his palm settling on my ribs. The goosebumps that rose in his wake, a purely topographical response to the thermal differential between his skin and the room's conditioned air.

There was no pretense of intimacy. He was not trying to connect with me. He was admiring a recent acquisition.

When he reached my breasts, he paused. He cupped one in his hand, weighing it with a connoisseur's focus. His thumb brushed against my nipple, and I watched it harden with the disinterest of a scientist observing a chemical reaction. He leaned down, his breath a warm cloud against my skin, and took the peak into his mouth.

The sensation was electric. A clean, uncomplicated signal from nerve to brain. My body, that proficient beast, responded as expected. A slight involuntary arch in my back. A quickening of my pulse. I registered these responses as data points. Stimulus: Oral. Response: Physical arousal. Emotional component: Null.

He moved between my legs, parting them gently. His focus was absolute. He was not looking at me. He was looking at the lines, the colors, the textures. His tongue, when it touched me, was a shock of heat and precision. It was the most technically proficient cunnilingus I had ever experienced, and the most soulless. It was an act of excavation, not of passion. He was a connoisseur tasting a rare vintage, identifying the notes, appreciating the complexity, but with no thought for the vine from which it grew. His tongue was a precise instrument, a metronome of sensation, mapping the ridges and folds with a dispassionate curiosity that was its own form of violation.

My mind, my fortress, remained serene. I cataloged his technique. I noted the way he used pressure and rhythm to build a predictable, mechanical response. My hips began to move, a motion I neither encouraged nor resisted. It was simply the body's physics taking over. The pleasure was a bright, sterile thing, like the focused glare of a light in an operating theater. It was happening to me, not with me.

I felt the climax approach, a wave of pure sensation gathering force. He felt it too, his efforts intensifying, his breathing growing ragged against my thigh. He was an artist determined to finish his work. The release, when it came, was a fracture. A neurological event. A shudder ran through me, a current without a soul, and then it was over. He had elicited the desired response. The sculpture had performed its function.

He rose, his face flushed with a victor's pride. He entered me without a word, his body a warm, heavy weight. His rhythm was steady, efficient. I stared at the pattern of the crystal vase on the nightstand, counting the facets as a meditative exercise, a way to anchor my consciousness outside the theater of my own body. I felt his body tense, heard the low groan torn from his throat. His release was an orderly, punctual affair. The transaction was complete.

He withdrew, tidied himself with a towel, and dressed. He placed a thick envelope on the nightstand. Cash. A deviation from my usual electronic payment preference, but one he had insisted upon for his own reasons of discretion.

"You are exquisite," he said, his voice once again the cool, distant tone of the appraiser. "A masterpiece."

I said nothing. The script required my silence. He left, and the door clicked shut with a soft, expensive sound.

I lay there for a moment in the deafening silence of the suite, the scent of sex and lilies hanging in the air. I felt nothing. Not disgust, not pleasure, not satisfaction. Just a profound blankness. I had been a beautiful object, perfectly appreciated. My thesis was proven once again.

I showered. The water was scalding, sluicing away the scent of him, the feel of him, the entire encounter. I watched the water bead on my skin, and I was myself again. I dressed in my own uniform: the black turtleneck, the tailored trousers. I became invisible.

I left the hotel, the envelope heavy in my satchel, and walked into the cool evening air. On the way to the subway, I stopped at an ATM, the machine's unfeeling glow a comfort in the dark. I fed the crisp bills from the envelope into the deposit slot; the machine swallowing them with a series of hungry whirs. My receipt printed on flimsy thermal paper, and I glanced at the new balance. The number was a string of zeros that represented a lifetime of security for most people. I stared at it, feeling the same utter blankness I'd felt in the suite. It was just data. A high score in a game, I was beginning to suspect I had already lost. I crumpled the receipt and dropped it in the trash, my mind already curating the entry. Sanitized. Academic. An ideal specimen of aesthetic hunger.

An hour later, I was sitting opposite Arthur.

The restaurant was a small, quiet Italian place in the Village he'd chosen. It was the antithesis of the Baccarat. It was warm, the air thick and humid, carrying the scent of garlic, yeast from baking bread, and the faint, sweet acidity of old wine. It was lit by candles whose flickering, living light made everyone look softer, kinder, and more real. It was a place designed for human connection, and every nerve in my body was on high alert.

Arthur was sixty-seven, with a kind, tired face and the tweed jacket of a retired professor. He had lost his wife of forty years to cancer six months ago. His request had been simple: dinner, once a month. "I just can't bear the silence of my own table anymore," he'd said on the phone, his voice thick with a grief so plain and unadorned it had bypassed all my defenses.

He was not a specimen. I had no idea how to categorize him.

He was easy to talk to. He spoke of his wife, Annette, with a gentle, smiling fondness. He told me about her terrible gardening skills and her love for bad detective novels. He wasn't asking me to be her, or to replace her. He was simply activating the muscles of memory, keeping her alive in the telling.

My role was simple. I listened. I smiled. I was Aura, the pleasant, beautiful canvas. I felt the soft complaint of the wooden chair beneath me, tasted the earthy note of the Chianti on my tongue, and kept my answers to his polite questions vague and professional. It was easy. It was safe.

"You know," he said, swirling the red wine in his glass, "Annette was a great reader. Voracious. Our house is… it's a fire hazard, really. Just stacks and stacks of books." He smiled at the memory. Then he looked at me, his gaze clear and direct, without a trace of the analytical chill I was used to. It was just… interest.

He set his glass down. "I'm sorry, I've been talking about myself all night. Tell me," he said, his voice gentle. "What do you like to read, when you're not working?"

The question landed in the center of the table and detonated.

It was not a question for Aura. Aura didn't read; she researched. Aura didn't like; she analyzed. Liking was a messy, subjective, emotional thing. Liking was for other people. Liking was for the girl I had buried. For Cassie.

My entire system short-circuited. It was a sudden system failure, a glitch in the code of my carefully constructed persona. My professional training, my years of curating the perfect response, all of it evaporated. My heart gave a painful, percussive thud against my ribs. The warmth of the room felt suddenly suffocating, the air too thick to draw into my lungs. I could feel the ghost of The Collector's touch on my skin, a cold, clinical memory. I could feel the violent, meaningless spasm of my own orgasm, a physiological event devoid of substance. I could feel the phantom weight of the cash I had deposited on the way to the restaurant, still in my bag. All of it was my armor. All of it was my fortress.

And this kind, sad old man had just walked right up to the gate. He was not wielding a battering ram, or any other siege equipment, but with a simple question, the entire structure threatened to collapse.

He was waiting for an answer.

I swallowed, the taste of acid at the back of my throat. I arranged my face into a pleasant, professional mask. I gave the answer that Aura would give.

"I'm mostly interested in art history texts," I said, my voice sounding impossibly distant. "Biographies of the great masters. That sort of thing."

It was the truth, but it was also a perfect lie.

Arthur nodded, oblivious to the war that had just been fought and lost in the space of a single heartbeat. "Ah, an academic," he said with a warm smile. "Annette would have liked you."

He went on talking, but I barely heard him. I had survived the moment. I had deflected. I had remained in control.

But as I sat there, across from this man who wanted nothing from my body and everything from a simple, human conversation, I felt a tremor of something I hadn't felt in years. It was a cold dread. The Collector had paid to turn me into an object for an hour, and it meant nothing. Arthur, with five simple words, had accidentally, yet completely devastatingly, reminded me I was a person.

And I realized my collection had a fatal flaw. I was the curator of cages, but I had never stopped to consider that the most perfect, most intricate, and most inescapable cage of all might just be the one I was looking out from.

CHAPTER 10

The Ghostwriter

After the encounter with Arthur, the silence in my apartment has changed its texture. It is no longer the cold polished steel of control. It is the brittle, thin glass of a vacuum chamber. I feel fragile inside it, as if a single noise can shatter everything. I need a client. I need to get back to the familiar, to the clean lines of a transaction. I need to prove that Arthur is an anomaly, no more than a statistical outlier in my data set.

The request that comes in is perfect. A referral from a client who values discretion and intellect. The job description is simple: "A living muse for a literary project." The pay is obscene. It feels safe. It feels like home.

His name was Derek, and his loft in SoHo smelled of whiskey, musty paper, and a faint, masculine arrogance I recognized as the cologne of my own tribe: the professional observers. The whiskey scent was not the warm invitation of a shared drink; it was the sour ghost of last night's inspiration, an acidic top note over the base of aging paper. The space was a curated performance of the writer's life. Towering walls of books possessed a funerary neatness, alphabetized by author. A vintage leather Chesterfield, its surface cracked into a beautiful, dishonest patina, sat opposite a gleaming Mac on a desk. Next to the computer, a purely decorative Underwood typewriter stood as a silent, impotent monument to a more authentic past. The light from the vast industrial windows was filtered through old, wavy glass, making the city outside seem like a shimmering, unreliable narrative.

"You must be Aura," he said, pouring two fingers of amber liquid into a heavy crystal glass without asking if I wanted one. His voice had a practiced, resonant quality. The voice of a man who listens to his own audiobooks. "Derek. Thank you for coming. I trust the project was explained?"

"To a degree," I said, placing my satchel on the floor. The dark polished oak floorboards felt unnervingly solid beneath my heels. I remained standing. "The details were… sparse."

"They are," he said with a thin, knowing smile. It was the smile of a critic who had already written the review. He gestured to the Chesterfield. "The project is an erotica novel. A commission. Good money, terrible genre. My agent thinks it's a smart commercial move. I think it's a necessary evil." He took a sip of his whiskey, his eyes assessing me over the rim of the glass. "The problem is, I'm a theorist. I can write about the semiotics of desire, the post-structuralist implications of a gaze, but the actual granular detail of it… the mechanics… it feels clumsy. False. A referral from our mutual acquaintance mentioned you were… methodical. That you had a researcher's eye. It's why I thought you'd be perfect. I don't need a performer; I need a collaborator. Someone to help me get the details right."

The hunger was a familiar one: a desire for authenticity, sub-contracted. I was to be his research department. I felt the cool confidence of the curator returning. I knew this specimen.

"I understand," I said, my voice settling into its professional, pleasant blankness. "What is the first scene?"

He picked up a Moleskine notebook. "The scene is simple. A man has hired a woman. He is an artist. She is his model. He wants to possess her, not just with his eyes, but with his words. He is going to narrate her, and in narrating her, he will own her."

A chill, thin and taut as a wire, traced its way down my spine. The sensation was a data point I registered and immediately tried to file away. It was just a story.

"He will describe what she is to do," Derek continued, his eyes fixed on me now, the writer's gaze sharpening into a scalpel. "And she will do it. Let's begin. Sit."

I sat on the edge of the indicated couch. The leather was cool and smooth, its surface seeming to resist the warmth of my body.

"Good," he murmured, and the soft click-clack of his keyboard began. It was not the sound of creation. It was the sound of tran-scription, a series of sharp, clinical reports. "The woman sat, her posture a perfect, elegant line. She was a professional. He could see it in the stillness of her hands, the deliberate lack of affect in her expression. She was a canvas, waiting for the first stroke of paint. Waiting for the first word."

He paused, his fingers hovering. "Cross your legs. Right over left."

I did. The movement felt slow, deliberate, as if moving through a medium thicker than air. I was an actress taking direction.

"She crossed her legs, the whisper of nylon a soft sibilance in the quiet room. A promise. He watched the taut line of her calf, the delicate curve of her ankle. Every part of her was a choice. Meticulous, curated. A collection of beautiful, defensive gestures."

My breath hitched. Curated. The word was not a slap. It was a stray bullet finding a target I did not know I was wearing. It was a password to my own operating system, spoken by a stranger. He couldn't know. It was just a lucky guess. A writer's intuition.

"This is where he begins to test her," Derek said, his voice a low murmur, his fingers never ceasing their rhythmic typing. "He wants to see if she is merely a performer, or something more. He wants to see the cracks in the porcelain." He looked up from the screen, his gaze pinning me not like a lover, but like an entomologist. "Take off your shoes."

I reached down, my movements fluid, and slipped off my heels. The gesture felt practiced, but my heart had begun a low, heavy drumming, a somatic dissent I struggled to contain. I placed them neatly on the floor beside me. The Persian rug was a soft, dense landscape under the balls of my bare feet. This was not like the Judge's interrogation, which had been a game of intellect. This felt... different. More invasive. He wasn't trying to break my arguments; he was trying to write my soul.

"She removed her shoes without a word. An act of submission so subtle he almost missed it. Now she was grounded, anchored to his space. The act changed the angle of her arch, the tension in her hamstrings. It made her vulnerable. It made her real."

"Stand up," he commanded, his voice still low, but with a new edge of authority that vibrated in the air. "Walk to the window."

I stood and walked across the rug. The city lights glittered beyond the glass, a million lesser lives arranged in a beautiful, meaningless grid. It was a familiar view from an unfamiliar cage.

"She moved with the grace of a dancer, her body a long, dark line against the city's electric glitter. He imagined the feel of the silk of her dress, the warmth of the skin beneath. He was building her in his mind, word by word." Derek's voice was closer now. I realized he had risen and was standing just behind me. I could feel the heat of his body, smell the whiskey on his breath, an acute, intrusive scent. He was another kind of academic vampire, I realized, one who fed not on ideas whispered in the dark, but on the living text of the body itself.

"Now," he whispered, his voice directly behind my ear, a violation of my personal airspace. "He tells her to undress. But he doesn't want to see her naked. Not yet. He wants to watch the process. The deconstruction."

My hands were cold. I reached behind my back for the zipper of my dress. My fingers, usually so certain, felt clumsy, alien, as if I were trying to pick a lock with the wrong tools.

"Her hands, so steady before, hesitated for a fraction of a second. There. The first crack. The first sign of the woman beneath the performance. The sound of the zipper was a surgical incision into the perfect seamless surface she presented to the world."

The dress pooled at my feet with a soft, liquid sigh. The cool air of the loft kissed my skin, raising goosebumps I could not catalog away. They were not a reaction to temperature; they were a topographical map of my own terror. I stood in my simple black lingerie, the same evidence I had presented to the Judge. But where she had seen an argument, he was seeing a confession.

He began to circle me, his fingers flying across a small tablet he now held. The clicking was faster, more urgent. "Her skin was pale, luminous in the half-light. A topography of control. He wanted to map her. To trace the line of her collarbone with his tongue, to feel the frantic pulse at the base of her throat with his lips. He wanted to taste her control."

He stopped in front of me. He did not touch me. But his words did. They were hands all over my body, stripping away my defenses, layer by layer.

"And now," he said, his voice thick with the narrative he was creating, "the artist touches the canvas." He reached out, and his fingers traced the lace edge of my bra. The fabric felt coarse against my overstimulated skin. My nipple hardened instantly, a traitorous, involuntary response, a piece of data I could not control.

He smiled a wolf's smile. "There. A reaction. Unbidden. Uncurated. The body telling a truth the mind wants to deny. He leaned in, his mouth hovering just over hers, and he whispered the next line of the story directly into her."

He leaned in, his lips brushing mine, a dry, warm pressure. The words he spoke were not for the novel. They were for me. "You're a researcher, aren't you, Aura? A collector. I can see it in your eyes. You think you're here to study me. But you're the most fascinating specimen I've ever had in my studio."

The floor dropped out from under me. He saw it. He saw the whole damn thing. The book, the collection, the sterile academic exercise of my life. He saw it, and he was turning it into pornography.

His mouth was on mine then, a hot, declarative kiss that was not a question but a verdict. And as he kissed me, he kept narrating, his voice a low, hypnotic rumble against my lips, my throat, my skin, a vibration that seemed to bypass my ears and enter my bones directly. He pushed me backwards until I felt the edge of the Chesterfield against the back of my knees. I sank back onto the leather, its coolness a shock against my bare thighs. His hands and mouth were an exploration, but his words were the real violation. He narrated my every reaction before it even happened, colonizing the space between sensation and my analysis of it.

"Her mind is screaming, fighting for control, for detachment, but her body… her body is arching into his touch, her hips lifting to meet his, a silent plea…"

And my hips lifted. My body, that Judas, obeyed his script.

"He finds her, wet and hot, a secret she can't hide, a story her body is desperate to tell…"

And I was. God help me, I was. My wetness was a humiliating confession.

He stripped away my underwear with a single, fluid motion as if he were turning a page. His mouth and fingers were a seminar in sensation, a relentless, academic exploration. One long finger slid inside me, hooking slightly, pressing against that hidden, nameless nerve while his thumb circled my clit with a maddening, metronomic rhythm. And all the while, he whispered. 'The slick heat of her, the way she clenches around my finger, a desperate, unspoken grammar…' His tongue replaced his thumb, a hot, wet, pointed thing tracing the seams of my flesh, dipping into the folds, tasting my surrender before I had even given it. All I could hear were his words, writing me, defining me, pinning me to the board like one of my own specimens. The pleasure was excruciating, a neurological firestorm inseparable from the horror of being so completely, utterly seen. He was inside my fortress, reading my private thoughts aloud.

The climax, when it came, was not a release. It was a surrender. A complete and total capitulation. My back arched off the leather, a silent scream caught in my throat as his name for me, Aura, echoed in my skull. It was a shuddering, sobbing orgasm that felt like a death, a vivisection of the soul. My mind was wiped clean of every theory, every defense, every cold, academic word I had ever used to protect myself as the convulsions took me, one after another, each one a nail in the coffin of my control. I was pure data being overwritten.

He rose from me, still fully dressed, his face flushed, his breathing heavy. He looked down at me, splayed on his couch, a wreck of a woman, a crime scene. He gave a small, satisfied nod. The artist, pleased with his work.

He walked back to his desk, sat down, and typed for another minute. The final soft clicks echoed in the ringing silence. The payment was already in my account. The transaction was complete.

I dressed in a daze, my body feeling alien, my uniform a costume that no longer fit. My skin felt... loud. I didn't look at him as I walked to the door.

"The chapter is finished," he said to my back. "Thank you for the... material."

I fled.

Back in my apartment, the silence isn't brittle glass anymore. It is a mirror. A two-way mirror. And for the first time, I feel like the one being watched. I sit at my desk and open the document for my book.

Specimen G: The Ghostwriter.

I stare at the title; my fingers freeze over the keys. How can I write about him? How can I curate a memory when he is the one holding the pen? He hadn't just bought my body for an evening. He has plagiarized my soul.

The smugness of the curator is gone. The thrill of the researcher is a joke. All that is left is the chilling, unthinkable question that his whole performance was designed to ask:

If the collector is collected, what is she worth?

CHAPTER 11

The Scholar's Gambit

After Derek, the silence in my apartment is no longer a curated space of control. It is an accusation. Every polished surface seems to reflect a version of myself I don't recognize, all splayed and undone on a stranger's couch, my own carefully constructed language used as a weapon against me. He took my method and turned it into a violation. He did not collect a specimen; he performed an autopsy on the collector.

I need to recalibrate. I need a transaction so clean, so purely within my own territory, that it scours the residue of his words from my skin. I scan my pending requests and find him. The perfect antidote. Dr. Edward. The request is for a single all-night session. The fantasy: an academic debate. The fee is substantial, but that isn't the lure. It is the subject line of his email: "A Meeting of Minds."

His apartment was in a crumbling pre-war building near the university I had fled, a detail that felt like a deliberate cosmic joke.

The air inside was thick with the ghosts of untold books. It was a particulate atmosphere, heavy with the slow, patient decay of paper, the fine grey dust of forgotten arguments settling on every surface. It smelled of that specific entropy, of stale pipe tobacco, and the bitter scent of intellectual pride that has begun to rust. Books were not just on shelves; they were in precarious, leaning towers on the floor, on the chairs, on the mantelpiece, their sheer mass seeming to suck the oxygen from the room. My fingers brushed a stack as I passed; the paper felt brittle, yielding, the dust a fine, gritty powder against my skin. The only sound was the faint, asthmatic wheeze of a radiator in the corner, a lonely mechanical sigh against the weight of so much silent text. It was a fortress of knowledge under siege from its own entropy.

Edward was in his late fifties, with a soft paunch straining against a worn corduroy jacket and a face that was a battlefield between intelligence and disappointment. Broken capillaries on his cheeks told a story of late nights and better whiskey than he could likely now afford. His eyes, magnified by thick glasses, were sharp, but the skin around them was puffy and tired. He was a man who had been formidable once.

I knew his story. Everyone in my former world knew it. A celebrated historian, a titan in his field, brought down by a scandal so pathetic it was less a tragedy and more a cautionary tale. The sin was beyond simple plagiarism, which would have been vulgar. It was a quieter, more ghoulish act. A sin of erasure. For thirty years, he shared a mind with another historian, a man named Allan Herbert. They were a unit, a fabled partnership. When Herbert died of a sudden aneurysm, Edward published their life's work, their shared magnum opus on the Medici, under his name alone. He systematically wrote him out of their shared history, claiming decades of collaborative discovery as his own solitary genius. He had not stolen a student's paper. He had stolen a dead man's ghost. The act of intellectual vampirism was the same, even if the victim was different.

The parallel to my own quiet exodus from that world was a resonance I chose to ignore.

"Aura," he said, his voice a dry rustle of pages. "Thank you for indulging me. A drink?"

"No, thank you," I said, setting my satchel down on a rare clear patch of floor. "Shall we establish the terms of the discourse?"

A flicker of a smile, condescending and practiced. "Of course. The proposition is simple. We debate. The topic, as agreed: 'The weaponization of the gaze in sixteenth-century Florentine portraiture, from Bronzino to Vasari.'"

My topic. The core of the thesis my mentor had absorbed into his own work, leaving me with nothing but the ashes of the ideas. The irony was a blade twisting in a wound I thought had long since healed. I had not simply found it by accident. I had seen it displayed in the university bookshop, his name, Professor Amos Hall, in elegant gold serif on the cover of a book… My book.

"The rules are as follows," Edward continued, pacing in front of his cold fireplace, his steps stirring small eddies of dust. "We will both disrobe. The argument is to be the only thing that clothes us. The first to concede a point, to fail in their rebuttal, or to be brought to a logical fallacy from which they cannot recover… loses."

"And the consequences of losing?" I asked, my voice a cool, level line, the acoustics of the book-crammed room giving it a dead, flat quality.

His eyes glided over my body for the first time, a flicker of something other than academic interest in their depths. "The loser, having been intellectually dominated, will then submit to the winner.

Physically. In whatever manner the victor sees fit. The mind, you see, is the primary organ. The body is merely the… spoils."

The hunger was for reclamation. He wanted to win back the intellectual authority he'd lost, and to consecrate that victory with a physical conquest. He saw me as a beautiful, intelligent prop for his own restoration. He had no idea he had just invited the ghost of a dead girl to her own funeral, and she had come ready to dance.

"I find the terms acceptable," I said.

We undressed with a strange, formal solemnity, as if we were dons removing our robes before a duel. The cool, dusty air of the apartment felt like a physical presence against my skin as the layers came away. His body was pale and soft, a scholar's body, a vessel for the mind it carried, with a faint geography of silvery stretch marks across his belly. I folded my turtleneck and trousers with my usual precision, placing them on a chair, a neat black altar in the chaos. I stood before him naked; my posture erect. The chill in the room was a welcome sharpening agent. I was not offering my body; I was sharpening it into a weapon. Exhibit A: The argument made flesh.

"Let us begin," he said, his gaze fixed on my face. Edward began his opening argument, but all I could hear was Amos. The scent of his office, dry sherry and Swisher Sweets, a paternal warmth I had mistaken for love. The intellectual intimacy came first, heady and thrilling. Then the physical, his hand on my back, his lips on my neck in the quiet of the stacks. He called me his brilliant girl.

"I propose that Bronzino's portraits, particularly of the Medici, are not merely representations of power, but are themselves acts of political aggression. The cold, enamel-like surfaces and the direct, unblinking gaze of his subjects serve to objectify and dominate not only the sitter, but the viewer. They are a declaration that you are being seen by your superior. Your opening rebuttal?"

I met his gaze, and for a second I saw Amos's tired disappointment, the look he gave me when I finally confronted him. He had not just stolen my words. He had harvested my life. The pillow talk, the half-formed ideas whispered in the dark after sex, all polished and presented as his own solitary genius. My footnotes had become his chapters. My voice, his legacy. The university's investigation had been a public execution. He was a tenured giant. I was a graduate student, his lover. The narrative was simple and brutal. I was not a scholar plagiarized. I was a woman scorned. Hysterical. My meticulous notes reframed as the obsessive work of a jilted assistant.

And so it began. For the next three hours, we wove a tapestry of argument and evidence. We spoke of Mannerist detachment and the Renaissance cult of personality. We debated the semiotics of a gloved hand, the symbolism of a prayer book held as a weapon. The air grew thick with our words, with the heat of pure, focused intellect, a tangible pressure in the small room.

It was intoxicating.

I had forgotten this feeling. The thrill of a perfectly executed thesis, the joy of marshalling facts into an unassailable fortress of logic. I felt the dormant parts of my mind waking up, stretching. The dust fell away. Cassie was at the lectern, and she was incandescent.

I watched Edward as I spoke, cataloging the flush that crept up his neck as I dismantled his argument about Vasari's courtly deference. I noted the slight tremor in his hand when I quoted a primary source he had clearly forgotten. And I saw with the dispassionate eye of the researcher, the slow, steady hardening of his cock. He was getting off on this. On the fight. On the proximity to the brilliance he had lost.

But I was getting off on it too. A different kind of arousal, a cold fire in my veins. The feeling of power. The joy of absolute competence. I felt a flush on my own skin, a somatic response to the pure, orgasmic thrill of being right. My pulse became a controlled variable, a steady percussive beat I monitored with detachment. The experience had taught me a valuable lesson. The observer holds all the power. The specimen has none. And so, I killed the specimen. I buried Cassie in that campus ground. In her place, I built Aura. A perfect, unfeeling observer.

The killing blow came four hours in. He was trying to argue for the inherent passivity of the female subject, using Lucrezia Panciatichi as his prime example. He was on unsteady ground, his argument sloppy, desperate.

I let him finish, a predator giving its prey a final, foolish dash for freedom. Then I moved in.

"You're fundamentally misreading the iconography, Doctor," I said, my voice soft, but each word a perfectly sharpened dart that cut through the thick, intellectual air. "You see passivity in Lucrezia's gaze. I see a carefully constructed prison of piety she is intellectually dismantling from within. The book in her hands isn't a symbol of her submission to God; it's a symbol of her access to a world beyond her husband, beyond Florence, beyond you. You see a beautiful object. I see a mind honing itself against the bars of its cage. Your entire premise is predicated on a sixteenth-century male gaze that you have failed to deconstruct. It is, if you'll forgive me, a disappointingly rudimentary error."

Silence. The word hung in the air between us. Rudimentary. The silence was not empty; it was a vacuum, and it sucked the life from the room.

It was over. I saw it in his eyes. The intellectual fire was gone, replaced by the flat grey of defeat. The erection he had sported for the last hour wilted, a flag of surrender. The flush drained from his face, leaving his skin looking papery and old. He looked… broken. A profound, shuddering sigh escaped his lips. The sound a man makes when the ghost of who he used to be finally leaves the room.

He had lost. And in his face, I no longer saw the client, but the ghost of my own mentor. The same entitled surprise. The same crumbling arrogance. The same pathetic defeat.

And the victory, the orgasm of the mind I had been chasing all night, turned to bile in my throat.

"I… concede," he whispered, the words sounding like they were dredged from the bottom of a well. He sank into a worn armchair, his soft, naked body looking defenseless and old. "The spoils… are yours."

I looked at him, this broken man in his fortress of decaying knowledge. My hunger for this transaction had been to feel the satisfying click of intellectual dominance. To re-establish my own control. But now, all I felt was a profound and hollow sadness. I had resurrected Cassie just to watch her brutalize a pathetic old man. We were two ghosts in a room, and one of us had just proven to be the crueler specter.

The script demanded I claim my prize. I walked over to him. I knelt before his chair on the dusty Persian rug. My movements were fluid, professional. This was the work. This was the transaction. I took his flaccid penis into my hand. The skin was cool and loose, like old parchment. I lowered my head and took him into my mouth, my motions skilled, efficient, and utterly devoid of feeling. I was a machine completing a task. The taste was faintly acidic, of shame. I focused on the precise mechanics of the gag reflex, the muscular control required, the way to use tongue and palate to simulate an enthusiasm I did not possess.

He made no sound. He just sat there, his head bowed, as I brought him to a sad, perfunctory climax that felt like a final, quiet punctuation mark on a life of failure. The taste in my mouth was not of sex. It was of regret.

I finished, tidied myself with a hand towel he had draped over a nearby chair for that purpose, and dressed. He didn't move from the chair.

I collected my satchel. The payment had been wired when I arrived. A perfectly executed transaction.

As I walked to the door, his voice, small and thin, stopped me.

"You're brilliant," he said, not looking at me. "Truly. What a waste."

I closed the door behind me without a word. The cold night air was a shock. I walked past the university library, its stone lions flanking the entrance like weary, soot-stained sphinxes guarding a tomb of dead ideas. A gust of wind sent a flurry of dry leaves skittering across the quad, a sound like ghosts whispering. It was a walk through a graveyard, and I was the only one who knew where all the bodies were buried.

I had won this round. I had dominated. I had proven that I was smarter, sharper, and better.

But all I felt was the truth of his final words. The words did not register as sound but as a physical touch, a hollow bruise just beyond my ribs. I had just performed a flawless autopsy on a part of myself I had sworn was dead, and the victory felt exactly like a loss. I had gone seeking control, but all I had found was the shape of my own cage, and the chilling realization that I had become its most willing, and most brutal, warden.

CHAPTER 12

The Perfumer's Ghost

After the Scholar, I craved a transaction of profound quiet. My mind was a battlefield littered with the ghosts of arguments won and lost, and the echo of my own name, Cassie, was a piece of shrapnel I could not dislodge. I needed a client who wanted nothing from my intellect, nothing from my past. I needed a blank space. A silence.

The request from Clint, the perfumer, seemed a perfect prescription. "To be the vessel for a memory." It was poetic, passive, and clean. I envisioned an hour spent sitting in a beautiful room, wearing a scent, a living piece of potpourri. An easy, lucrative reset.

His studio, however, was not a space of quiet contemplation. It was a library of smells. Hundreds, perhaps thousands, of small, dark glass bottles were arranged on shelves like a mad apothecary's dream, their labels handwritten in a spidery, obsessive script. The air was not a singular, pleasant fragrance but a dense, complex chord of conflicting notes. It had a physical weight, a humidity that seemed to coat the inside of my lungs. The sharp green promise of galbanum fought with the narcotic sweetness of tuberose, while the dirty, animalic hum of civet warred with the clean, almost holy scent of frankincense. It was overwhelming, a direct assault on the senses that bypassed my intellectual defenses entirely. Scent is a brute-force entry into memory, a key that requires no lock. I felt a sudden profound vulnerability, as if the air itself was reading the corrupted files of my mind.

Clint was a man made of gentle frayed edges. He had kind, bloodshot eyes and long, elegant fingers stained with amber oils. He wore a linen shirt that was soft with a hundred washings, and he moved with the slow, careful grace of a man navigating a world made of glass. His grief was not a cloak he wore so much as the atmosphere of the room itself.

"Aura," he said, his voice a soft rasp. "Thank you. I know this is… unusual."

"I specialize in the unusual," I said, my professional mask clicking into place, a familiar and welcome weight.

"It's not just to wear her perfume," he said, gesturing to a single, empty crystal flacon on a workbench. The bottle was a beautiful faceted tomb. "That bottle is all I have left of it. The scent is gone. Faded. The formula… she made it herself. It was her. I've been trying to rebuild it for a year." He looked at me, and his gaze was one of such raw, desperate hope that I had to look away. "The problem is, you can't test a fragrance on paper. Not really. Paper has no life, no heat. A perfume needs skin to bloom. To tell its story. I need… a blank page."

I was the page. The hunger was not just for a memory; it was for a resurrection. He wanted to use my living chemistry to bring his wife back from the dead for an hour. The sheer beautiful horror of it was compelling.

"I understand," I said.

The ritual began. He asked me to undress. I did so with my usual unhurried efficiency, folding my clothes into a neat black square. I stood before him, a clinical specimen. But he was not looking at my body with the appraising eye of the Collector or the intellectual curiosity of the Judge. He was looking at my skin as a medium. A canvas.

"We start with the base notes," he whispered, his voice taking on the hypnotic cadence of a priest. He took a glass dropper and drew a bead of dark, viscous oil. "Oakmoss. Because she was grounded. She had roots." He came to me, and his touch was feather-light, impersonal, as he dabbed the oil onto the pulse point of my left wrist. The scent was cool, earthy, like a forest floor after the rain. The oil itself was cool too, a single drop of liquid shadow against my skin, and I felt my pulse give a small, startled leap beneath his touch, a somatic dissent I immediately cataloged and dismissed.

He returned to his workbench. "And sandalwood. For her warmth." He applied it to my right wrist. The scent was creamy, woody, a soft, enveloping heat that seemed to radiate through my veins, a thermal signature spreading from the point of contact. He did not speak to me, but to her. To the ghost he was summoning in the air between us.

My mind raced to catalog, to analyze. Olfactory memory association. Subjective emotional response projection. The limbic system, a primitive and unreliable narrator. But the words were meaningless. My skin was tingling where he had touched me. My own chemistry was already reacting, warming the oils, changing them, making them mine.

"Now, the heart," he murmured. He chose a new bottle. "Tube-rose. For her laughter. It was… dangerous." He applied this one to the sensitive skin in the crooks of my elbows. The scent was a narcotic blast of white floral, so sweet it was almost carnal. It felt heavy in my lungs, a beautiful poison. I felt a strange, languid heat begin to pool in my belly, a purely physiological response to the indolic compounds, nothing more. My body, that stupid, faithful animal, was responding to the story he was telling.

He moved behind me. I felt the warmth of his body close to my back, but he did not touch me. "And a touch of jasmine. For the nights." His fingers, cool and dry, brushed the nape of my neck as he applied the oil. I shivered, an involuntary response that felt like a betrayal, a glitch in my programming. The jasmine was heady, indolic, the scent of sex and secrets, a fragrance that did not suggest intimacy so much as demand it.

He was building her on my skin, note by note. He was not touching me for pleasure, yet it was the most intimate act I had ever endured. My body was no longer my own. It was a vessel, a haunted house, and the ghost was beginning to wake up. My nipples hardened, the peaks aching against the cool, heavy air; my breath grew shallow. I was becoming aroused by the cartography of a dead woman's soul.

He stood before me again, his eyes unfocused, looking through me to her. "The top notes," he breathed. "This is what you noticed first. This was the introduction." He took a dropper of pale golden oil. "Bergamot. For her wit. It was bright, and sharp, and could make you smile before you knew why."

He leaned in. His focus was absolute. He dabbed the oil onto the hollow of my throat. I could feel his breath on my skin, warm and smelling faintly of tea and sorrow. He stayed there for a moment, his face inches from mine, his eyes closed. The microscopic sound of his linen shirt whispering against his own skin was an unbearable intrusion. He was not breathing me in. He was breathing her in.

"That's it," he whispered, a sound of unadulterated agony. "Oh, god. Livia. That's it."

A single tear escaped his eye and traced a path down his cheek. He did not seem to notice. He was lost. He leaned closer, his nose tracing the air along my collarbone, down to the valley between my breasts, where the heart notes of tuberose and jasmine were blooming with my body's heat. He was not a client. I was not an escort. He was a man, and I was the shape of his wife, and in that moment, the love he felt for her was a physical force in the room. It was a pressure, a heat, a wave that washed over me, through me.

And my fortress, already cracked and compromised, was obliterated.

My body, which I had curated and controlled and offered as a sterile object for years, made a choice without me. A deep, shuddering tremor ran through me, starting in my feet and racing up my spine. The combined scent of the oils, the heat of his grief, and the sheer unbearable intimacy of being the object of such profound, hopeless devotion. It was too much. The arousal, which had been a slow, confusing burn, ignited.

A low gasp escaped my lips, a sound I had not authorized. My body, the one thing over which I had absolute dominion, was staging a coup. My back arched, my hips pushed forward in a single involuntary motion, a gesture with no author. He was still inches away, lost in his spectral reunion, as the climax tore through me. It was not my own. It felt like a foreign signal, a violent electrical impulse that used my muscles, my nerves, my throat to express a pleasure that belonged to a ghost. My system was overloaded, rebooting in the ruins of a feeling I had no name for. It was an orgasm of pure empathy, a beautiful piece of data I could never classify.

He pulled back, his eyes slowly focusing on me, on the flush on my skin, my ragged breathing. He saw me, Aura, for the first time. A flicker of confusion followed by shame crossed his face.

"I… I'm sorry," he stammered, taking a step back.

I could not speak. I was undone. Violated not by a man's touch, but by the sheer unshielded force of his love for another.

I dressed in a fog, my hands shaking. The scent of his wife, of Livia, was now my scent. It clung to my skin, a beautiful, suffocating shroud. I collected my satchel. The payment was in cash on the table. A neat transaction.

I walked out into the night, and every person I passed, every gust of wind from the street, felt like an intrusion.

Back in my apartment, the silence does not rush in the way it usually does. The scent fills the space before it can. The bathroom is a continuation of the apartment's theme. Floor-to-ceiling slabs of grey marble, a walk-in shower with a frame-less glass door that is invisible when clean. On the counter, there is a single, unscented bar of white soap in a square dish. In a recessed cabinet, a stack of identical white towels, folded with military precision. It is a space for decontamination, not for primping. And tonight, it has utterly failed. I shower for an hour, the water scalding, a frantic, useless attempt at exorcism, but I cannot wash it off. It is in my hair, on my skin, and in my head.

Afterward, I sit at my desk, the white light of the monitor carving my face from the darkness. I open the document.

Specimen I: The Perfumer's Ghost.

I place my fingers on the keys, ready to curate, to catalog, to pin the memory to the board with the sterile, academic language that has always been my shield.

But no words come. How can I describe his hunger when, for a few shattering moments, I was consumed by his love? How can I analyze the transaction when my own body has offered a response I did not authorize; a messy, shuddering, unwanted piece of data that invalidates the entire experiment?

I close the laptop. In the dark, I lift my wrist to my face and breathe in.

Oakmoss. Sandalwood. Tuberose.

It smells like a memory of a life I have never lived. And for the first time, I feel the terrifying, hollow ache of the space where a love like that is supposed to be. The collection is no longer a source of control. It is becoming an index of my own ghosts.

CHAPTER 13

The Cartographer

For three days after the Perfumer, I live inside a ghost. The scent of Livia clings to my skin, a beautiful and torturous shroud I can't scrub away. The silence of my apartment is no longer my own; it is hers. I catch myself turning, expecting to see someone, and the person I am expecting has her face, a face I have never even seen. My control, my fortress, has been taken by a phantom army, and I am in full panicked retreat.

I need to reclaim my own skin.

That's why I choose Evelyn. The request is a balm of intellectualism. "To be charted. A topographical survey of the human form." It is a female client. The fantasy is abstract, bloodless. It feels safe. It feels like the perfect sanitized environment to conduct a controlled burn, to incinerate the ghost of Livia and re-establish my own borders.

Her apartment, a penthouse overlooking the river, was not a home. It was an observatory. The air had a dry, archival quality, smelling of old paper, beeswax, and the faint, metallic scent of electricity from the humming electronic globe in the corner. Antique brass telescopes, their lenses like predatory eyes, were aimed at the sky. Framed celestial charts and ancient, hand-drawn maps covered the walls, their faded ink a testament to a thousand forgotten coastlines. It was a space dedicated to the art of knowing, of pinning a thing to a grid and giving it a name. I should have recognized the danger immediately.

Evelyn was in her fifties, with a severe silver bob and the piercing, intelligent grey eyes of a hawk. She wore a tailored silk pantsuit the color of a stormy sea, the fabric making a soft, liquid whisper as she moved. She moved with a frictionless precision, as if she were gliding along a pre-plotted course.

"Pleasure to finally meet you Aura," she said, her voice a low, melodic hum that seemed to vibrate in the room's profound quiet. "Welcome. The terms are understood?"

"They are."

"Good." She gestured to a large, low platform in the center of the room, draped in a sheet of dark, star chart blue velvet. The fabric seemed to swallow the light, its texture deep and soft as a new bruise. "You will disrobe and lie on your back. You will not speak. You will not move unless instructed. Your only function is to be the landscape. My function is to be the explorer. Is that clear?"

"Perfectly." The word was my armor clicking back into place. I was a professional. This was a script I understood.

"Before we begin," she added, her voice a low, melodic hum, "a note on methodology. The best cartographers always survey the terrain before an expedition. One must understand the history of a place, its previous names, its forgotten ruins. It is the only way to create a truly accurate map."

I undressed with my practiced, fluid grace, folding my black uniform into a neat square. I was Aura, the blank canvas, the beautiful object. But as I lay back on the velvet, its surface cool as a crypt against my skin, a tremor of something unfamiliar skittered across my skin. Apprehension. For the first time, I felt like a specimen before the session had even begun. A chill, colder and more specific than the air in the room, traced its way down my spine. This was not a fantasy. This was a threat.

Evelyn approached, holding not a whip or a rope, but a single silver fountain pen, its nib retracted. The cap came off with a quiet, definitive click. It was an instrument of definition. She knelt beside the platform, her movements unhurried. Her stormy grey eyes weren't looking at my body as a source of pleasure; they were assessing it as a problem of geography.

"The survey begins," she whispered, more to herself than to me.

She started with my left hand, taking it gently. Her fingers were cool and dry. She extended my fingers. The tip of the pen, a cold and perfectly smooth point of polished metal, touched the base of my palm.

"The Five Estuaries," she murmured, her voice a hypnotic current. She traced the line of my index finger from knuckle to tip. "The First River. We will call it… Patience." The pen moved over my skin, a cold, deliberate fire, leaving a trail of goosebumps in its wake. My mind, my fortress, scrambled to do its work. Specimen J: The Cartographer. Hunger: Epistemophilia, the love of knowledge, eroticized. A desire to possess through definition.

The analysis felt thin. A paper shield against a rising tide.

She traced the next finger. "The Second… Pride." I felt a flicker of detached admiration for her metaphors even as the clinical intimacy of her touch began to feel invasive.

She moved to my arm, her touch still impossibly light. The pen's tip circled my wrist bone. "The Isle of Grace." Her own finger replaced the pen, pressing lightly into the pulse point. I felt my own blood beat against her touch, a frantic, trapped bird hammering against the cage of her fingertip. "And beneath it, the Hidden Spring."

I focused on my breathing. In. Out. I was a researcher. I was in control.

She moved upwards, her attention absolute. Her free hand rested on my hip, a cool, proprietary weight that seemed to claim the territory even before she named it. The pen traced the elegant line of my collarbone. "The Ridge of Sighs," she breathed, her voice close to my ear. I smelled the clean scent of her perfume, something with vetiver and ink. I fought the urge to shiver. The name was too close to a truth I kept locked away, a reference to the sighs I cataloged in others but never allowed myself.

This was the violation. Of sovereignty rather than flesh. She was doing to my body what I did to my clients' minds in my book. She was observing, naming, and curating me. Pinning me to her board. The role reversal was so absolute, so precise, it felt like a surgical procedure performed without anesthesia.

Her hand slid from my hip to the flat plane of my stomach. "The Pale Plains of Silence." The pen's tip circled my navel, a slow, deliberate vortex. "The Sunken Well." My abdominal muscles clenched involuntarily. A reaction. Unbidden. A crack in the porcelain.

This is the work, I told myself. This is the transaction. But my body, that treacherous creature still haunted by the Perfumer's ghost, wasn't listening. A slow, liquid heat was beginning to pool between my legs, a humiliating response to this cold, intellectual conquest. I was getting wet from the sheer terrifying intimacy of being so completely seen.

She moved lower, and my breath caught in my throat. Her hand brushed the inside of my thigh, the fine hairs there standing on end, and the skin erupted in a riot of sensation. "The Velvet Slopes," she murmured, her voice dropping an octave. The pen traced the crease where my thigh met my hip. "The Boundary Line."

She parted my legs with a gentle, inexorable pressure. I was exposed. The air in the room felt suddenly arctic on my wet folds. My heart was a frantic fist pounding on the walls of my chest.

"And here," she whispered, her voice now a thread of awe, "the final territory. The Uncharted Interior."

Her finger, not the pen, traced the outer lips of my sex. The touch was not erotic; it was geological. I bit my own lip to keep from making a sound. My hips gave a small, traitorous buck. I was losing. The landscape was experiencing a seismic event.

"A complex delta," she analyzed, her touch impossibly precise. "Guarded by the Twin Sentinels." Her thumb found my clitoris, a small, hard pearl of pure nerve hidden in the folds. It brushed once, a flick of fire, and I gasped. The sound was ripped out of me, a breach in the dam, a violation of the primary rule.

Evelyn smiled, a faint, triumphant curve of her lips. It was the quiet satisfaction of a researcher confirming a hypothesis. "Ah," she said. "A tremor. The land is… alive."

She didn't touch my clitoris again. That would have been too simple, too crude. Instead, she leaned in, her mouth hovering over the valley between my breasts. I could feel the heat of her breath. She didn't kiss me. She spoke.

"I see it," she whispered, her voice sinking into my very bones. "The core of this continent. The source of all its rivers and all its silence. The thing it protects."

Her finger moved from my thigh and settled on the small, soft space just above my pubic bone. A place no one had ever touched with such intention. A place that felt like the keystone of my entire being. She pressed down, a single, knowing point of pressure.

"I was on the acquisitions committee for the university press that year," she murmured, her voice a thread of cool steel. "I read his manuscript. *The Gaze as Governance.* A brilliant, if derivative, work. And in the acknowledgments of the first draft, there was a footnote. A thank you to a promising research assistant for her 'invaluable contributions' to several core concepts. A footnote that mysteriously vanished in the final printing." She paused, letting the weight of the revelation land. "He named her, and then he erased her. The most elegant thefts always leave a ghost. We will call this place… Cassandra's Hope."

My name.

My real name.

The word was a key turning a lock I had forgotten existed. It was not a guess. It was a verdict. In that moment, I knew. She had researched me, had excavated the ruins of my former life from the academic wreckage, perhaps a forgotten footnote in my mentor's stolen work. The entire session had been a trap. A flawless, beautiful, horrific trap.

The orgasm was a shattering. A fault line rupturing down the center of my curated self. My back arched off the velvet, a silent scream caught in my throat as my own name echoed through the corridors of my mind. It was a violent, full-body cataclysm that had nothing to do with pleasure and everything to do with being found. Convulsions wracked my body, wave after wave of utter, soul-stripping surrender. I was not an explorer. I was a land being claimed, named, and conquered, flayed open by a single word.

When the last tremor faded, I lay there, soul bared, tears streaming silently into my hair. The heat of my own release was a foreign, swampy climate on my skin.

Evelyn rose, her composure absolute. She looked down at me with the quiet satisfaction of a scholar whose life's thesis had just been irrefutably proven.

"The survey is complete," she said, her voice cool and melodic once more. "You are now a known world."

I dressed in a daze, my limbs feeling disconnected, my own clothes a stranger's costume. The payment was wired to my account as I stepped out the door. A complete transaction.

Back in my apartment, the key feels alien in my hand, a tool for entering a space that is no longer my own. The silence is not the sanitary polished steel of my design. It is the vast, humming silence of an observatory after a new, terrible star has been discovered. It is Evelyn's silence.

I walk to the western wall of glass. The city sprawls below, a vast circuit board of light, its grid of streets and avenues a perfect, terrifying echo of the lines she had just drawn on my own skin. The glass does not keep the city out; it holds it in, a silent, captured specimen, and tonight, I am just another part of the collection.

I move to stand before the mirror, but the reflection is a foreign country. I do not see Aura's curated perfection or Cassie's wounded intelligence. I see a map, a feverish atlas of newly named territories. I see the Ridge of Sighs, the Pale Plains of Silence, and the devastating, newly charted territory of Cassandra's Hope. Her words are etched over my own skin. I am a known world.

A soft weight brushes against my ankle, a silent inquiry. Klio looks up at me, her green eyes blinking slowly, two unnamed, uncharted points of light in the gloom. She gives a small, questioning meow. It is a sound with no subtext, no theory. It is a simple biological fact.

I scoop her into my arms, my body desperate for a weight that is not my own. The simple, living heat of her is a shock. She is a warm, purring engine against my chest, a low, somatic rumble that resists all analysis. I bury my face in her soft black fur, inhaling the simple, animal scent of her. She smells of dust and sleep and life. She does not know my name. She does not care about the Ridge of Sighs. My collarbone is simply a convenient ledge for her head. My stomach is a warm place to knead her paws.

I sink to the floor, my back against the wall, holding her tightly. The vibration of her purr is a current of pure, uncurated life in the sterile tomb of my apartment. She is the only thing in this entire, newly mapped world that has no name for my parts. She is the only thing that is still mine.

I hold her until my arms ache, a living anchor in the terrifying sea of my own geography. I walk to my desk to write the entry, to reclaim the narrative. But my fingers hover over the keys, useless. How can you be the author when you have already been written?

CHAPTER 14

The Blank Page

The shower is a tactical failure. I stand under a stream of water hot enough to feel like an abrasion, a punishment. I am scrubbing my skin with a loofah until it is raw, a frantic attempt to physically exfoliate the phantom cartography Evelyn etched beyond my epidermis, somewhere deeper, a palimpsest on the soul. The steam is a blinding white fog, a temporary erasure of the room around me, but it cannot obscure the map inside my head. *The Ridge of Sighs. The Pale Plains of Silence. Cassandra's Hope.* The names are a relentless internal whisper against the roar of the water. The soap I use is unscented, a sterile chemical lie against the phantom scent of Evelyn's perfume, a fragrance of vetiver and ink I can still smell on my own wrists.

I dry myself with a brutal efficiency and pull on the uniform. The black turtleneck feels different tonight. Its familiar, suffocating softness is not a comfort. It is a mourning shroud for a woman who never got to live. I need to work. The work is the cure. The work is the process by which chaos is ordered, by which messy, volatile human experience is captured, pinned, and rendered inert under the cold light of analysis. The work is the only thing that is real.

Klio, a small, black, fuzzy question mark, winds herself around my ankles, her purr a low living engine in the vast silence of the apartment. This silence is different. It is no longer the polished steel of control. It is the silence of a library after a fire, the air thick with the ghosts of burned words. Her silent inquiry is a pinprick of simple biological reality in my complex intellectual crisis.

I feed her. The ritual is a small and steadying anchor in a tide of vertigo. The sound of the dry kibble rattling into the ceramic bowl. The soft wet noise as she eats. These are simple, classifiable data points. Predictable. Safe. I run a hand down her back, the silk of her fur a brief, startling truth against my fingertips. She does not know my name. She does not care about the Ridge of Sighs. She accepts my touch without theory.

Then, I walk to my desk. The cool, lacquered wood is a familiar altar. The white rectangle of the monitor carves my face from the darkness once more. The familiar ritual. The summoning of the curator.

I open the document. The cursor blinks at the end of the last entry, a steady, patient, mocking pulse. A tiny, digital heartbeat measuring the seconds of my paralysis. I hit enter, creating a clean white space for the new specimen. The blankness on the screen is not a promise of potential. It is an accusation. It is a mirror reflecting the new, terrifying emptiness inside me.

My fingers, usually so precise, so certain on the keys, feel like foreign objects, thick and clumsy. I place them in the home position. I take a breath, the air tasting of the room's sterile quiet. I begin the process. The curation.

I type the title.

Specimen J: The Cartographer.

The words look obscene on the page. A lie. A profound and unforgivable misattribution of the primary role. I am not the cartographer. I am the uncharted territory that has been ruthlessly, exquisitely mapped. I am the specimen. My entire taxonomy has collapsed.

My fingers freeze. The academic language, long since my scalpel and my shield, will not come. How can I describe her hunger to possess through definition, when my own definition has been stolen? How can I analyze the session with clinical detachment when I am still lying on that blue velvet platform, my own name a brand on my skin? The memory is not a clean data point. It is a somatic ghost, a phantom pressure on my collarbone, a remembered chill on my exposed skin.

I try again. I force the words. *The subject, Evelyn, exhibits a classic epistemophilic desire, eroticizing the act of knowing...*

The words are chalk in my mouth. They are a foreign language. They are the language of the old life, the life of the observer. But I am no longer observing. I have been seen. The two-way mirror has been shattered, and I am standing in the glittering, sharp-edged debris, bleeding. The system has crashed. The observer and the subject have merged, and the data is hopelessly, irrevocably contaminated by the self. And without clean data, what is the thesis? What is the point?

The cursor blinks. Blink. Blink. Blink. A tiny digital god of time, measuring out the seconds of my failure. I am a researcher whose experiment has turned on her.

A low growl of frustration escapes my throat, a sound I do not recognize, a feral dissent from the body I have tried so hard to silence. I slam the laptop shut. The light dies, plunging the room into absolute darkness. The silence that rushes in is no longer an ally. It is a sensory deprivation chamber of my own making. A room with no doors. A cage whose bars are built from Evelyn's words, from my own name.

I sit there in the dark, my pulse loud in my ears, a frantic animal drumming against the walls of my chest. The intellectual framework has failed. The analysis is useless. The words are gone. All that is left is the body. The landscape. The raw, screaming, unclassified territory of the self, still humming with the phantom touch of the Somatic Detective, still aching with the ghost of Arthur's kindness.

And in this moment of absolute intellectual failure, I know what I need. I need a transaction with no words. No history. No names. I need a client who wants nothing but the body. A simple, brutal, physical act that will cauterize this wound. A session of pure mechanics, a somatic scream so loud it will obliterate thought. A reset to the factory settings of flesh and force.

I need to feel control, even if it is just the simple, primal control of a hand holding a hammer.

CHAPTER 15

The Mechanism of Failure

The recent encounters had escalated from haunting my senses to dissecting my history. I pace the sterile confines of my apartment, the plush rug a silent grey desert under my feet, but there is no escape from the residue they have left behind. I can still feel the phantom trace of their conclusions, the echo of my own name spoken by a stranger, a cartographer's brand on my very soul. They have not just touched me. They have documented me.

Control. I need it back. Not the smug intellectual control of the early days, but a primal, physical, undeniable control. I need a transaction so simple, so rooted in the body, that it will cauterize the wound Evelyn has left with the clean, white heat of a purely mechanical act. I scan my active requests, my fingers flying across the screen, searching for an antidote, for a specimen whose needs are beautifully, blessedly uncomplicated.

And there he is. Specimen K. The Watchmaker. His request is a haiku of submission: "To be an object. To be restrained. To be used. No words."

It is perfect. A pure power dynamic. A return to first principles. I am not going to be a map or a ghost or a character in a novel. I am going to be the hand that holds the hammer.

His workshop was on a quiet cobblestone street downtown, a place where time itself seemed to slow to the patient tick of an escapement wheel. The air did not smell of ambition or grief; it smelled of brass, lubricating oil, and patient, oiled wood. It was a room filled with innumerable tiny, intricate mechanisms, a sanctuary of precision. Magnifying glasses on articulated arms loomed over benches where infinitesimally small gears and springs lay in velvet-lined trays like sleeping insects. The silence here was not an absence, but a presence, a dense medium in which the only acceptable sounds were the tiny clicks of a world being put in perfect order. I understood him instantly.

He was a small, neat man in his forties, with a watchmaker's loupe still attached to his glasses and hands that were steady and immaculate. He did not meet my eyes. His gaze was fixed on a point on the floor just to my left, a man already ashamed of the beautiful, simple truth of his hunger. He wanted to be broken down into his component parts. He wanted, for one hour, to stop ticking.

"The… materials are prepared," he whispered, the words barely disturbing the dusty air. He gestured to a sturdy, wooden armless chair in the center of the room. On a small table beside it, four lengths of thick, black leather cord were coiled with obsessive precision.

"You will remove your clothes," I said, my voice the familiar, cool instrument of Aura. The sound of it settled me, a welcome and necessary calibration. "You will not sit in the chair. You will sit on the floor and straddle its legs, facing its high back."

He obeyed with a shuddering sigh of relief. This was his release: the relinquishing of choice. This position served a dual function: it presented his back to me as a landscape of submission, while also splaying his legs, a geometry of forced vulnerability. As he settled onto the floor, his chest pressed against the wooden slats of the chair back, he was a supplicant at an altar of his own making. I felt the first flicker of my old power returning. This was my gallery. This was my lab.

I began with his wrists, securing them in front of him, binding them to the upper spindles of the chair back. The leather was thick and smelled of tannin, stiff in my hands before it yielded. It groaned a soft, protesting sound as I pulled the knots tight, a sound I cataloged as a satisfying note of compliance. His arms were stretched tight, pinning his upper body to the chair. He was immobilized, an object of study.

The ankles came next, secured to the front legs of the chair. The angle was precise, designed to lock his hips in place and prevent any retreat. He was now a living sculpture of submission, his body pale and vulnerable amidst the complex machinery of his life. His head was bowed, his breathing shallow and rapid. He was ready. I removed my own clothes and walked around behind him, my bare feet silent on the wooden floorboards, my own nakedness a statement of my power in this room. I was the one who was free.

I placed my hands on his shoulders. The skin was cool and tight over the dense muscle, a landscape of contained anxiety. My thumbs pressed into the knots beside his spine, seeking the familiar trigger points of release, a cartography of tension I knew by heart. I could feel the frantic, shallow beat of his heart through his skin, the thrum of a machine wound too tight. My job was to provide the release valve.

But my mind was a traitor. As I traced the line of his spine with my fingers, a phantom chill traced the line of my own collarbone. *The Ridge of Sighs.* Evelyn's voice was not a memory; it was a nerve ending firing, a cold and precise echo inside my own skin. My touch, which should have been deliberate and focused, felt disconnected, the gesture of an automaton.

I knelt behind him, the floorboards cool and solid beneath my knees. My hand slid down his back, over the curve of his ass and across his hip, and cupped him from behind. He was already hard, his cock a rigid, desperate thing straining against his belly. The heat of him was a shock against my cool palm. He flinched at my touch, a full-body tremor of anticipation.

"You wanted to be an object," I whispered, my lips close to his ear, the words tasting as though I had licked an old ashtray. I was speaking to him, but I was arguing with her. "An object has no will. An object only feels what it is made to feel."

My fingers wrapped around his shaft. His skin was hot and velvety. I began to stroke him, my rhythm slow, mechanical. I was a piston. A gear. I was giving him exactly what he had paid for. But I felt nothing. The satisfying hum of control I expected was absent. In its place was a high, thin ringing in my ears. The sound of a vacuum.

His hips began to move, a desperate, silent plea. He wanted more. He wanted to be used. I moved to the front of the chair to face him. His legs were parted by the bonds, his vulnerability absolute. I straddled the chair itself without sitting, my knees on either side of the seat, bringing my cunt level with his mouth, hovering just inches from his face. I could feel the heat radiating from his skin, smell the clean, metallic scent of his arousal. I leaned down and took his cock in my hand again, my other hand tangling in his hair, pulling his head back. I wanted to see his face. I needed to see the surrender in his eyes to feel my own power.

But when I looked at him, I did not see a submissive. I saw a specimen pinned to a board. And in the reflection in his glasses, I saw my own face, my expression not of dominance, but of stark, hollow-eyed panic.

Cassandra's Hope.

The name detonated behind my eyes like a flashbulb, bleaching the room white for a second. My rhythm faltered. My grip tightened too hard. He winced. It was a small, broken sound escaping his lips. A professional dominant would have used that sound, woven it into the scene. I barely registered it. I was a million miles away, lying on a blue velvet platform while a woman with stormy grey eyes rewrote my soul. My heart began a frantic, panicked drumming against my ribs, a broken machine inside me.

"Please," he gasped. The single word was a violation of our contract, but he was a drowning man begging for air. He could feel me slipping away. He could feel the fantasy dying.

The sound of his voice snapped me back. I was failing. I was failing at the one thing I could not afford to fail at. With a surge of desperate, angry energy, I pushed him to the edge. My stroking became fast, brutal, efficient. I was no longer a dominant orchestrating a scene; I was a mechanic trying to force a stalled engine to turn over. His body tensed, his back arched, and with a guttural, choked cry, he came, his release a hot, messy spasm against my hand.

The transaction was complete.

But as I stood wiping his semen from my hand with a cloth from his workbench, there was no sense of victory. No smug satisfaction.

Only the sour, metallic taste of my own failure. He was slumped in his bonds, breathing heavily, but his release had felt like a desperate, lonely affair. I had been a ghost in the room.

I untied him, my movements quick and impersonal. He did not speak, just huddled, rubbing the circulation back into his wrists, the red marks from the leather a temporary stigmata. As I dressed, pulling on the familiar black armor of my turtleneck, he finally looked at me. His eyes were not full of grateful submission. They were full of a gentle, pitying concern.

"Are you alright?" he asked, his voice soft. "You seemed… far away."

The words were a slap. A hot physical blow. I had just been paid an obscene amount of money to perform, and the client was asking if I was okay. The shame was a physical heat that flooded my face, so intense it felt like a fever. I had not been a mirror for his hunger. I had been a window into my own brokenness.

I took the envelope of cash from the bench and left without a word.

The cold night air does nothing to cool the burn in my cheeks. I have gone seeking control and have only proven how completely I have lost it. I do not go home. I cannot face the silence of that apartment, a space that now feels mapped and named by another. I walk, my feet carrying me to the one place in the city that feels real, the one place that smells of stories instead of ghosts.

The bell above Arlo's bookbindery chimes, a sound like a distant friendly memory. The warm air, thick with the scent of paper, leather, and binding glue, wraps around me like a blanket, a sanctuary from the sterile rain.

Arlo is at his workbench planing the edge of a book board. He looks up over his spectacles, his shrewd, kind eyes taking in my too-pale face, the slight tremor in my hands. He does not smile.

"Cassie," he grunts. He is the only one. The name does not feel like an attack from him. It just feels like a fact. "You look like… well, you look like hell."

"Just a long night," I lie, my voice thin.

He sets his plane down and wipes his hands on his apron. He gestures with his chin to the stack of pristine, cream-colored pages on his desk. My pages.

"Brought me any new entries for the collection?" he asks, his gaze steady.

I cannot answer. I cannot begin to articulate the pathetic, failed transaction I have just fled. I cannot write about the Watchmaker, because the story is not about him. It is about me.

He knows. Of course he knows. He leans back, his stool groaning, and crosses his thick arms.

"You know, kid," he says, his voice dropping into that low, gentle rumble he saves for when he is about to tell the truth. "I've been looking at these pages you bring me. The Architect. The Judge, the Perfumer. It's beautiful work. The writing is impeccable. Precise." He picks up a finished sheet, the one detailing the Photographer's chilly studio. He holds it up to the light. "But it's all so cold. Colder than a morgue. All these people, all these hungers…"

He puts the page down, and his eyes, clear and kind and utterly without judgment, find mine. He holds my gaze, and for the first time all night, I do not feel like a specimen. I feel like a person.

"I asked you once where you were in all this," he says, his voice so quiet I have to lean in to hear it. "I was wrong to ask. You're on every single page. You're the cage, Cassie. This whole damn book is the blueprint for the cage you built for yourself. My only question now is, when are you going to realize you're the one holding the key?"

CHAPTER 16

The Widower's Gift

*A*rthur was a data set I could not quantify. He was the anomaly in my collection, the specimen that refused to stay pinned to the board, a statistical error that threatened to corrupt the entire system. After the Watchmaker, after Arlo's quiet, damning question, the thought of our scheduled dinner was not a comfort. It was an existential threat. My other clients were a mirror; Arthur was a window, and I had spent the last several years bricking up every window in my life. I considered canceling. A sudden illness. A family emergency. The professional, sterile lies came easily, a familiar and tasteless balm. But I did not. Some perverse, self-destructive part of me, the part that had survived the academic abattoir, needed to walk back into the fire to prove it could not be burned.

I armored myself in the usual way. The black silk blouse, a softer version of the turtleneck, felt like a second skin, its frictionless surface a promise of no attachments. Trousers tailored with precision, a clean line against a messy world. My hair was tied back so tightly it pulled at my temples, a pleasant, focusing pain that helped to sharpen the edges of the Aura persona. I was composed. I was expensive. I was blank. I walked into the warm, garlic-scented chaos of the Italian restaurant, the heat of it a physical shock after the cool night air. The clatter of silverware and the murmur of a dozen undocumented lives were a cacophony against my internal silence. I found him already at our table, a quiet island of tweed in a sea of boisterous humanity.

"Aura," he said, his eyes crinkling in a smile that was so devoid of artifice it felt like a sudden drop in cabin pressure, a sensation that knocked the wind out of me. "You look lovely."

"Arthur," I replied, my own smile a careful, calculated curve I felt pull at the corners of my mouth. "You're looking well."

The dinner proceeded along its usual placid lines. He spoke of his late wife, Annette, not with the raw grief of the Perfumer, but with a gentle, companionable fondness, as if she were merely in the other room. He told a story about her disastrous attempt to bake bread that had ended with the fire department making a courtesy call. I performed my role. I listened. I smiled, my facial muscles held in a state of pleasant neutrality. I kept my internal monologue on a tight leash, cataloging his gestures, his choice of words, the way the flickering candlelight softened the lines of loss around his eyes and caught in the thinning silver of his hair. I was the researcher. I was safe.

But tonight, there was a new current in the air. A tension. He was watching me, too. Not with a client's gaze, but with a quiet, searching intensity. It was the look of a man trying to solve a puzzle, and it made the skin on my arms prickle.

"You seem… tired tonight," he said, swirling the Chianti in his glass. The deep red liquid coated the sides, a slow, viscous slide I tracked with my eyes, another data point.

"It's been a busy week," I said, the deflection smooth and automatic, a pre-recorded message from the Aura operating system.

"I'm sure." He paused, his gaze unwavering. "You know, for someone who makes their living with people, you've built a rather formidable wall around yourself."

The observation, so casual, so accurate, landed like a stone in the pit of my stomach. My training screamed at me to pivot, to turn it back on him with a charming professional parry about the nature of his own grief. But the words would not come. I felt a flush creep up my neck, a hot, shameful wave of exposure, a somatic event I could not catalog away. The heat from the small candle on our table suddenly felt like a spotlight.

"I'm a private person," I managed, the words feeling thin and brittle against the rich texture of the room.

He just nodded, a gesture of acceptance, not judgment, which was somehow worse. And then he reached down to the satchel at his feet.

"I know this is against the rules," he said, his voice soft. He placed a small rectangular package wrapped in simple brown paper and tied with string on the table between us. "But I saw it, and I thought of you."

A gift. Brown paper. String. A breach. A violation. A bomb. My entire system went into shock, a cascade of silent alarms. Rule number one in this profession, the unspoken rule that underpinned all the others: the transaction is the only thing that passes between us. Money for time. Presence for a fee. Nothing more. A gift implies a relationship. A gift is a seed from which attachment grows like a weed, choking out the clean, sterile lines of the professional.

"Arthur," I said, my voice tight, cold. "I can't accept this."

"Please," he said, his gaze open, pleading. "Just open it. If you still feel that way after, I'll take it back. I promise."

My hands were shaking. I, who could tie a man to a chair and bring him to ruin without a flicker of emotion, was trembling because of a brown paper package. My fingers, usually so precise, fumbled with the knot in the string. The brittle texture of the paper was an abrasive insult under my fingertips. The paper tore.

It was a book.

A slim volume, its cover a faded forget-me-not blue. I knew the feel of the binding, the specific weight of the old, thirsty paper, before I even read the title. It smelled of a life I had never lived, a faint, sweet dust of old vanilla and time. It was a first edition. A 1958 printing of *Bonjour Tristesse* by Françoise Sagan.

Three months ago, during our second dinner, he had asked what I liked to read. I had given him the safe, Aura answer: art history texts. But he had pressed gently, and I, in a moment of catastrophic carelessness, had mentioned a fleeting fondness for the "cool, detached prose of the French female existentialists." I had named Sagan. I had not thought he was even listening.

He had listened. He had remembered. He had searched.

This was not a gift for Aura. Aura did not have a fondness for anything. This was a gift for Cassie.

I stared at the book, at the elegant, faded font of the title. Sadness. Hello, sadness. I felt a hysterical laugh bubble in my throat like a toxic gas. I swallowed it down, but the pressure behind my eyes was immense, a physical ache.

"I… thank you," I whispered. The words felt like they were being pulled from me with forceps, each syllable a small, painful extraction.

"You're welcome, Cassie," he said.

The name. He had said it. Not by accident. Not as a slip. It was a statement. The name was not a sound. It was a physical collision, an ache just behind my ribs.

"Arthur, this is... how?" I whispered.

He smiled, a gentle, slightly sad expression. "Our mutual friend, the bookbinder. Arlo. I've been a customer of his for twenty years. He is the only bookbinder in the city who still practices the old craft. I used to take him my wife's first editions when they began to outlive their bindings. The man is an absolute miracle worker when it comes to restorative work. A few years ago, I was in his shop when he was processing a large collection of academic texts he'd just bought. He seemed troubled by it. He mentioned they'd belonged to a brilliant young scholar from the university who was forced out by some... academic politics. He said it was a crime, throwing away a mind like that." Arthur's gaze was direct and full of a profound, uncomplicated kindness. "He mentioned her name was Cassie. And when you mentioned Sagan a few months ago, I just... put it together. I hope this isn't an overstep."

He had said the name as a fact, unearthed by a chain of quiet decency. The name was not a weapon. It was a key, offered gently, to a door I had forgotten was there.

I stood up so abruptly my chair scraped against the floor, the sound a shriek in the warm hum of the restaurant. The entire room seemed to fall silent for a moment, and I felt a hundred pairs of eyes on me, a new and unwelcome kind of observation. "I have to go."

"Wait," he said, his voice still gentle. He stood, placing a hand on my arm. His touch was warm, dry, paternal. It was the first time he had ever touched me. It was an inferno. The heat of it was a trespass, seeping through the thin silk, a thermal signature that bypassed all my firewalls. "Don't run. Please. Just... one more hour. My apartment is just around the corner. We can have coffee. That's all."

I should have said no. I should have walked out, blocked his number, and burned the memory of this night from my mind. The streetlights were a smear of hostile gold through the restaurant window, a world of strangers where I could be safely anonymous. But I was no longer in control. The fortress had been breached, the warden was in shock, and the prisoner, the messy, terrified, brilliant girl I had kept locked in the dungeon for a decade, was rattling the bars of her cage. Every step was a negotiation between the drilled-in protocols of Aura and the frantic, chaotic impulse of the prisoner in the basement.

I nodded. A single curt, involuntary motion.

His apartment was exactly as I had pictured it, a complex archive of a shared life. It smelled of books, lemon polish, and his wife. Her presence was everywhere: in the faded chintz of the armchair, the silver framed photos on the mantelpiece of a smiling woman with his eyes, and the half finished knitting project still in a basket by the fire, the needles holding a stitch in the middle of a row, a life paused but not erased. It was not a sterile space of ambition or a curated gallery of grief. It was a habitat. A home that had lost one of its two hearts.

He made coffee, his movements slow and comfortable in his own space. I stood in the center of the living room, clutching the book to my chest like a shield, the sharp corners digging into my ribs. I felt like an alien. An intruder in this quiet, sacred place.

He handed me a mug, its ceramic surface radiating a gentle warmth. Our fingers brushed. I did not flinch. I was too far gone for that.

"I'm not trying to complicate things," he said, his kind, tired eyes full of a truth I could not bear to look at directly. "I just… I miss my wife. I miss talking to a smart, beautiful woman. And you are both of those things. But Aura is a ghost. I find myself wanting to talk to the person inside the ghost."

He took a step closer. The air between us was thick, electric with all the things my rules were designed to prevent.

"Tonight," he said, his voice dropping to a near whisper. "I don't want to hire Aura. I want to pay for an hour of Cassie's time. And I have a different request."

My pulse took off at a dead run. Here it was. The turn. The true hunger, revealed. I braced myself for the specific, pathetic, or strange details. My internal catalog spun, searching for a file that did not exist.

"I want you to lie down with me," he said.

My mind went blank.

"On the bed," he continued, his voice steady, though I could see a tremor in his hand as he set his coffee mug down. "Fully clothed. No sex. I just… I haven't held anyone in a year. I want you to hold me. And I want to hold you. Until the hour is up."

Of all the requests in my collection: the strange, the violent, the pathetic, the sublime, this was the most obscene. The most terrifying. There was no script for this. No power dynamic to analyze. It was not a performance of intimacy. It was just… intimacy.

I followed him to the bedroom in a daze. It was dominated by a large four-poster bed, covered in a worn floral quilt, a landscape of faded flowers, soft with a thousand washings. It smelled of lavender and cedar and a long and happy marriage. This was their bed. The thought was an intrusion, a violation of a space I had no right to enter.

He took off his shoes and his tweed jacket and lay on top of the covers, his back to me. He looked small, a grey-haired man in a sea of faded flowers. An invitation. A challenge.

My body moved without my permission. I slipped off my heels, my bare feet sinking into a plush, worn rug. I lay down on the bed beside him, my body an unyielding line of pure theory, a stiff, straight line of terrified muscle. The silence in the room was deafening. It was not my silence, the polished steel of control. It was a warm, breathing silence, full of ghosts and memory and the frantic, unsynchronized beating of two human hearts.

After a moment that stretched for an eternity, he rolled onto his side to face me. He reached out and placed his hand on my waist in a simple, anchoring weight.

"Is this okay?" he whispered.

I could not speak. The word was a foreign country. I just nodded.

I turned to face him. And then I did the bravest, most foolish thing I have ever done in my life. It was not a decision made in the command center of my mind. It was a coup staged in the blood and bone. I closed the distance. I slid my arm around his back and rested my head in the hollow of his shoulder. He smelled of coffee and clean warm laundry. The rough texture of his shirt was an abrasive reality against my cheek. He smelled like a person.

He let out a long, shuddering sigh, the sound I had heard from so many of my clients. The sound of a man relinquishing a weight. And then his arms were around me, holding me with a desperate, grateful tenderness that was not asking for anything in return.

We lay there, two strangers, two lonely people, holding each other in a dead woman's bed. And my fortress, my collection, my carefully curated life, all crumbled to dust. My body betrayed me completely. The first tear was a treachery, a hot, saline mutiny that escaped my eye and soaked into the worn cotton of his shirt. It was followed by another. And another. It was not a performance. It was not a curation. It was a series of silent, shuddering quakes that seemed to emanate from a place deep beneath the foundations of the fortress I had built. I was just… falling apart. And he just held me. Tighter.

When the hour was up, we untangled ourselves without a word. I sat up, my face a wreck, my armor in ruins around me. He placed the envelope with my fee on the nightstand. The sight of it was a profanity, a cheap souvenir from a holy site.

I walked to the door, the book still clutched in my hand, its corners digging into my palm.

"Cassie," he said.

I stopped, my back to him.

"Thank you."

I fled into the night, the book a cold, hard rectangle against my chest.

Back in my apartment, I do not turn on the light. I walk to my desk and sit in the dark, the silence rushing in to fill a space that is no longer empty, but hollowed out. I look at the beautiful hand-bound leather book Arlo made for me. My collection. My thesis. My fortress.

Arthur's gift is not a book. It is a Trojan horse, delivered straight through my gates. And as I sit here, I can feel the soldiers spilling out, silent and armed. The soldiers are not storming the gates. They are already inside. They have been here all along. And they are finally, finally, opening the door from within.

CHAPTER 17

The Forger's Elegy

Arthur's gift is an open wound. It sits on my nightstand, a small blue rectangle of truth in a life built from exquisite lies. *Bonjour Tristesse.* Hello, sadness. It is more than a book. It is a quiet, ticking explosive device. For three days, I circle it like a suspicious animal, the ghost of his touch a warm unwelcome brand on my arm, a somatic data point I cannot erase. My control, my meticulously curated silence, is poisoned by simple, unadorned kindness.

I need an antidote. I need a session so steeped in artifice, so dedicated to the beauty of the unreal, that it will cauterize the raw, bleeding edge of that encounter with the clean, white heat of performance. I find him in my inbox, a request so perfectly aligned with my needs it feels like a prayer answered by a devil I know well. *Specimen L: The Forger.* He wants a model for a "lost" Modigliani. The fee is a poem. The fantasy is a fortress.

His studio was a hushed, dusty chapel in a forgotten corner of the West Village. It smelled of turpentine, old wine, and the sweet decay of drying linseed oil. The air itself had texture, a fine particulate haze of pigment and time that seemed to slow the light, making it thick and golden like amber. It was not the sterile, brutalist space of Julio the photographer. Julio had captured reality. This man, Greg, invented it. Canvases in the style of Schiele and Klimt and Degas leaned against the walls. These were not copies; they were echoes, letters written to ghosts in a language of breathtaking fluency. They were magnificent, soulful lies.

Greg was a man of soft movements and clear, intelligent eyes. He had the long, ink-stained fingers of a calligrapher and a smile that understood the value of a beautiful secret. He poured two glasses of deep red wine without asking, the liquid a dark, viscous blood in the heavy crystal.

"To the muse," he said, his voice a low, conspiratorial murmur that did not echo in the sound-dampening clutter of the room. He did not look at my body. He looked at the way the light caught the line of my jaw, the specific geometry of shadow beneath my cheekbone. "And to the beautiful untruths that make life bearable."

I felt a wave of relief so profound it was almost dizzying. This was my language. This was my tribe. The wine tasted of dark cherries and dust, a flavor both earthy and decadent, and I let the warmth of it settle in my belly like a temporary truce. He was not a grieving widower or a pathetic tech bro. He was a craftsman. A fellow curator of illusions.

"The pose is specific," he said, gesturing to a simple wooden stool against a backdrop of raw, umber-colored linen. The fabric was coarse; its color the shade of dried blood. "The neck, long. The head, tilted. One arm behind the back, to elongate the torso. It will be uncomfortable. That discomfort is part of the line."

I understood. I undressed, folding my black silk blouse and trousers into their customary neat square. My body was my instrument, and I was a virtuoso. The cool air of the studio was a familiar lover, raising a fine map of goosebumps on my skin, a purely physiological response I cataloged and dismissed. I took the pose on the hard wooden stool, my spine a rigid column, my muscles protesting with a low, familiar burn I welcomed as a sign of control. I tilted my head, offering him the swan-like curve of my neck. I was not a woman. I was a shape. I was an idea. I was safe.

He began to sketch, the sound of the charcoal a dry, rhythmic whisper on the textured paper, a secret being told in a language without words. The silence stretched, comfortable and professional. I cataloged the room, the dust motes dancing in the slanted afternoon light, the precise arrangement of his brushes in a green ceramic jar, their bristles stiff with the ghosts of old colors. My mind was doing its work. *Specimen L: The Forger.* Hunger: to possess beauty by recreating it. A classic Pyglmalion variant.

Then, he began to speak.

"Modigliani was not a painter of portraits," he said, his eyes never leaving my form, a dark, consuming focus that felt more intimate than any touch. "He was a sculptor who used paint. He wasn't interested in your likeness. He was interested in the rhythm of your soul."

His gaze traced the line of my collarbone. My skin tingled where his eyes rested, a phantom touch that was more invasive than a hand. "He would see this not as bone, but as a phrase of music. A long melancholic note." The charcoal whispered. "Your eyes… he would paint them blank. Not because you are empty, but because the interior life is too vast to be rendered. It must be suggested. A beautiful, hollow space for the viewer to fall into."

A tremor, small and deep, started in my belly. My intellectual framework was beginning to dissolve in the acid of his perception. He was not describing a painting. He was describing my life, my entire professional thesis. He was describing Aura. The beautiful, hollow space.

He put down the charcoal and picked up a brush, dipping it into a pool of sienna. "A good forger does not copy," he continued, his voice a hypnotic caress. "A copy is a dead thing. A mimicry. A forger must understand the master so completely, so intimately, that he can dream a new work into existence. He must create a painting the master would have painted." A ghost of a memory, hot and shameful, surfaced. Amos Hall, scribbling my whispered pillow talk onto a legal pad. My brilliant, brilliant girl. Greg's words were a horrifying absolution for my mentor's crime. "It is not an act of deception. It is an act of profound, obsessive love."

He took a step closer, dabbing a test of color onto a palette. The scent of the oil paint was sharp and intoxicating, a clean chemical fire in my lungs. "To create the perfect forgery," he whispered, his voice sinking into my very bones, "you must find the lie the original artist was telling, and you must tell it better. More beautifully. You create an illusion that is more true, more pure in its intent, than the real thing."

My skin was on fire. My nipples were hard, aching points against the cool air. A slow, liquid heat was pooling between my legs, a humiliating, traitorous response. The arousal was not a simple biological event. It was a symptom of a profound intellectual violation. He was not touching me. He was dismantling me. Word by word.

He looked from the canvas to me, and his sharp eyes saw everything. The flush on my skin, a betraying tide of color rising on my throat and chest. The shallow flutter of my breath. The lie of my composure stretched taut and thin as a drumhead.

"You understand, don't you?" he said, his voice dropping, becoming the only sound in the universe. "The sheer, exquisite pleasure of the perfect performance. The art of becoming an illusion so complete, so beautiful, it feels more real than the person you left behind."

The breath I was holding escaped in a ragged gasp. He saw it. He saw the whole damn thing. The Client Book. The sterile apartment. The black uniform. He saw Aura, the magnificent, soulful lie I had painted over the messy, inconvenient truth of Cassie. The fortress was not under siege. He had simply walked through the front gate, holding the original blueprints.

His brush hovered in the air. "The most beautiful forgeries," he said, his voice a final, perfect cut, "are the ones we make of ourselves."

The session ended an hour later. The painting was a marvel, a long, elegant woman with a tilted head and sad, almond eyes that were beautifully, terrifyingly blank. He paid me in cash, an envelope thick with the scent of old paper. A complete transaction.

I walked home in a fog, the city a blur of meaningless light and noise.

Back in my apartment, the silence is a judgment. I stand before the mirror and see her. The long neck. The tilted head. The curated and perfect emptiness in the eyes.

I look at the small blue book on my nightstand, the real, tangible object from Arthur. Then, I look back at my reflection.

My collection is built on a single, elegant thesis: I am the curator of other people's hungers. But Greg, the forger, holds up a different kind of mirror. And in it, I am forced to face the question that now threatens to burn my entire collection to cinders.

Am I the artist? Or am I just the masterpiece of my own fraud?

CHAPTER 18

The Demolition Man

I choose the next client the way an addict chooses a fix. It is not a choice made with the cool curatorial mind of Aura. It is a panicked and desperate act of self-medication. The Forger has shown me the hollowness of my own artistry. Arthur has shown me the terrifying warmth of a life I have abandoned. I am a ghost caught between two mirrors, and I need to feel the satisfying, uncomplicated reality of something solid breaking. The sound of a structure failing is the only music that can drown out the quiet, insistent whisper of my own name.

His name was Robert, and his request was a single, elegant sentence: "I want you to help me burn my life to the ground."

His office was on the eighty-second floor, a cathedral of chrome and black leather that worshiped at the altar of capital. The air was pressurized, scrubbed so clean it had a sterile, chemical bite. It smelled of expensive carpet cleaner, the faint tang of fear, and the dry, ozonic hum of immense electronic power held in silent check. He was a man in his late forties, with a perfectly tailored silk and woolen Ralph Lauren suit, and the haunted, exhausted eyes of a king who knows his reign is a gilded prison. He had the kind of power that could move markets, but he couldn't move the deadweight in his own soul.

"Aura," he said, his voice a low, tight hum of anxiety that was a dissonant chord in the room's crushing quiet. "The payment has been confirmed. The building is empty. We have until dawn."

"I understand," I said. I placed my satchel on the floor, the soft leather making no sound on the plush beige wall-to-wall carpet. I walked to the center of the room. I was the instrument of his release. Tonight, there would be no soft architecture, no intellectual debate. Tonight, I was a natural disaster in a little black dress.

He gestured to the corner of his vast mahogany desk. A commercial-grade paper shredder, the size of a small engine, was plugged into the wall. Beside it were two dozen banker's boxes, filled with what I assumed was the entire paper trail of his professional life. Contracts. Memos. Reports. The architecture of his cage.

"We begin here," he said.

I did not need further instruction. I walked to the first box, my heels sinking into the plush carpet. I pulled out a thick sheaf of papers, the letterhead bearing the name of a multinational corporation I read about in the journals Marc, the Architect, favored. The paper felt heavy, important, its cotton fibers dense with consequence. I fed the first page into the shredder.

The machine roared to life with a hungry grinding sound that vibrated through the floor and up my legs. It was a violent, satisfying noise. The paper was annihilated, turned into a confetti of meaningless strips that rained into the bin below, releasing a fine, chalky dust into the air that smelled of processed wood pulp and hot metal. Robert let out a sound, a half sigh, half groan. I looked at him. He stood by the floor to ceiling window, his back to me, but I could see the tension in his shoulders. His erection was a hard, distinct ridge against the fine wool of his trousers in the reflection on the massive window.

This was the foreplay.

I worked with a steady, metronomic rhythm. I fed the machine his life, page by page. With every roar of the motor, the tension in the room coiled tighter. My own body responded, a low, electric hum starting in my veins. This was power. This was control. A thought, acute and unwelcome as a shard of glass, pierced the noise. It was Evelyn, the Cartographer, and her voice was a cold whisper in my mind. Had she found my name in a footnote of my mentor's stolen work? Was the ghost of my academic life so easy to Google? I shoved a thick financial report into the shredder with more force than necessary. The machine groaned, the pitch of its motor dropping for a moment, and then chewed it to pieces. I would not be documented. I would be the one who erases.

When the last box was empty, the fine dust of paper hung in the air, catching the city lights in a hazy, particulate cloud. Robert turned from the window. His face was flushed, his breathing shallow. He pointed to a glass shelf lined with crystal awards. Heavy, sharp-edged things engraved with his name.

"Now," he breathed. "Those."

I picked up the first one. It was surprisingly heavy, its faceted edges cold and sharp against my palms. A testament to his success. I held it for a moment, then I turned and hurled it against the opposite wall. The sound was a gunshot, a clean, explosive crack followed by the musical, cascading shatter of crystal raining onto the carpet.

Robert cried out, a raw, beastial sound of pure release. I picked up another. And another. I was a machine of destruction. I smashed his triumphs, his accolades, his carefully polished history, until the floor glittered with the debris. The shards looked like diamonds under the recessed lighting, a carpet of beautiful, dangerous jewels. With every crash, his arousal grew. He was breathing in ragged gasps, his hand clutching the front of his trousers, his knuckles white.

The real violence, however, was saved for last. He walked to his desk and turned the large monitor toward me. It showed a screen of neatly organized files. The digital archive. The soul of the company.

"Everything," he whispered, his voice thick with a desire so profound it was almost holy. "Delete everything."

I sat in his expensive leather chair. It was still warm from his body, holding the ghost of his shape. My fingers flew over the keyboard, the soft clicks a counterpoint to the savage chaos I had just unleashed. Select all. Are you sure you want to permanently delete these items? The question was a beautiful, final profanity. I clicked yes.

As the progress bar filled, erasing a lifetime of work in a silent, bloodless massacre, Robert came undone. He fell to his knees beside the desk, his head bowed, and a long, shuddering orgasm ripped through his body. He came in his thousand-dollar suit, a silent, messy offering to the god of oblivion. The transaction should have been complete.

But it wasn't.

He wanted to be the final thing that was broken. I stood, and he took my place, draping himself face down across the desk, scattering the few papers that remained. His silk trousers and designer briefs were already around his ankles. His ass was pale and vulnerable in the stark office lighting. He was offering himself to the storm.

He looked up at me, his face a ruin of sweat and release and desperation. "Now," he choked out. "Ruin me."

The request was a prayer for annihilation. A permission slip for the violence he craved. I came around the desk and walked right past my satchel sitting quietly near the opposite chair. My toolkit would not do for this request, though it contained perfectly adequate tools. My eyes scanned the glittering debris on the floor and found what I needed: the heavy base of a crystal award, its top sheared off, leaving a cylindrical shaft well-suited to the task. I picked it up. It was cold and brutally solid. There was no seduction. There was no tenderness. This was the aftershock.

The crystal base of the award was heavy in my hand, a brutal, solid thing. As I stood over Robert's prone form, the scene dissolved, the expensive office melting away into the dusty, sunlit confines of a university study.

I was standing in front of Professor Amos Hall's desk. In my hand was not a crystal weapon, but a sheaf of pages. The galley proofs for his book. My book.

"It's a simple question, Amos," I said, my voice preternaturally calm. My heart was a cold, terrified bird beating against my ribs. "Chapter three. The section on Bronzino's use of material culture as a signifier of political impermanence. Where did you get it?"

He looked up at me, his face a mask of weary, paternal disappointment. It was the look he gave undergraduates who had failed to grasp a basic concept. It was a look designed to make me feel small.

"Cassandra, my dear," he said, his voice the warm, familiar rumble that had once felt like home. "All scholarship is a conversation. We build on the ideas of others. You and I, we've had so many wonderful conversations."

"This was not a conversation," I said, my voice shaking now. "This was a monologue. My monologue. You've lifted entire paragraphs. My footnotes are your primary sources. You took the words we spoke in bed, the ideas I was still working on, and you published them under your name."

He sighed, the sound of a patient man dealing with a difficult child. He took off his glasses and rubbed the bridge of his nose. "You are a brilliant girl, Cassie. But you are emotional. You are seeing conspiracy where there is only collaboration. You gave me those ideas. Freely. As a student. As... a friend."

The word friend was a slap.

"I was your lover," I said, the words tasting like poison. "And I was your research assistant. And you have committed the most profound and cowardly theft I can imagine."

His face hardened then. The paternal warmth vanished, replaced by something cold and hard. The look of a king whose authority had been questioned. "Be very careful what you say next," he said, his voice dropping to a low, dangerous whisper. "You are a graduate student with a reputation for being... intense. I am a tenured professor with a sterling career. Who do you think the department will believe?"

I looked at him, at this man I had adored, this man who had been my intellectual everything. And I saw him for what he was.

A vampire. A forger. A man who had built his beautiful career on the bones of other people's brilliance. He had stolen years of my work without a single shred of guilt.

The memory shattered, and I was back in the high-rise office, the air thick with the smell of sex and destruction. I looked down at Robert, kneeling before me, offering his own ruin. And a cold, clean rage, the rage I had swallowed in that dusty office so long ago, flooded my veins. This man would pay for Amos's sins.

I spit on my hand, a primal, contemptuous gesture not for him, but for the weapon. I slicked the blunt end of the crystal and then his opening with two fingers, the invasion rough and immediate. He gasped, his hips bucking against the unyielding wood of the desk. Positioning the cold blunt base of it against him, I entered him with a single, brutal thrust, gripping the crystal base like a cock of my own. He screamed into the leather of his desk blotter, a sound of agony and ecstasy that was swallowed by the eighty-second floor silence.

I fucked him. I fucked him with all the cold, controlled rage that had been building in me for weeks. I fucked him with the ghost of Arthur's kindness and the acid of the Forger's truth. I was not a lover. I was a piston. I was a demolition machine. Each thrust was the smash of another crystal award, the roar of the shredder, the finality of the delete key. The friction of his body was an abrasion, the resistance of his flesh a satisfying, solid fact. The cold crystal warmed inside him, a parasitic heat. This was not sex; it was erasure, and I was fucking him with the ghost of my own ruined fortress.

He met my rhythm, his body a writhing, desperate thing, begging for its own annihilation.

His climax was a frantic sobbing affair, a complete system failure. He collapsed onto the desk, spent. I pulled the shaft out of him and dropped it to the floor, where it landed with a heavy, dead thud on the carpet. My own body was humming, a sterile, joyless pleasure echoing in my bones, leaving a metallic taste of adrenaline in my mouth.

I dressed in the wreckage of his life. He did not move. He just lay there, a pathetic, broken king on a throne of his own making. I took the envelope of cash from his jacket, which was draped over a chair near the door. Another completed transaction.

I walked out, leaving him in the glittering, paper-strewn darkness. The city lights were a cold, indifferent glitter as I descended. The thrill of the demolition, so potent and intoxicating, was already fading, replaced by a profound, chilling emptiness.

Back in my apartment, the silence is absolute. My space is pristine. Unbroken. Every object is in its place. I walk to my desk and look at the book Arlo made for me. My collection. My perfect unbreakable object. My beautiful suffocating cage.

The vicarious thrill from earlier was not a release at all. It was a rehearsal. And as I stand here in the sterile quiet of my own life, I feel the seductive urge to pick up a hammer.

CHAPTER 19

The Triptych

After the demolition, the pristine silence of my apartment is a physical threat. It is the silence of a perfectly preserved tomb, and the acrid aftertaste of Robert's desperation lingers on my palate. I had stood in the glittering wreckage of a man's life and felt a certain seductive envy. He burns it all down. I just go home and feed the cat.

I need noise. I need artifice. I need a performance so demanding it obliterates the memory of Arthur's simple, devastating kindness and the lingering scent of desperation. I need a client that is pure surface, a transaction of such dazzling, hollow beauty it reaffirms my faith in the unreal.

Their request has been sitting in my inbox for a week, a single, lacquered black invitation, hand delivered by messenger. The cardstock was so thick and dense it felt like a shard of polished stone, the font a severe, elegant silver. Kenneth and Ari. Their faces are an inescapable part of the city's visual landscape. I have seen them on billboards for perfume, their bodies intertwined in a monochrome lie of eternal passion. I have seen them in magazines for watches, their wrists touching in a pantomime of shared time. Their impossibly perfect marriage is the subject of numerous soft-focus articles. The request is for a single night at the Mark Hotel. The fantasy is unstated but implicit in their fame: to be a third panel in their perfect, public triptych. I accept. It feels like hiding in plain sight.

Preparation is a ritual. I begin with research, not into them, but into their brand. I spend two hours online, a researcher falling down a rabbit hole of curated perfection. I triangulate data points from paparazzi photos and staged interviews, mapping the geography of their public-facing intimacy. I scroll through a hundred photos of them on red carpets, their smiles perfectly angled, his hand always proprietary on the small of her back, a gesture of ownership disguised as support. I read three interviews, one in Vogue, two in Vanity Fair. The language is a symphony of artifice. They speak of "synergy," of "shared aesthetic values," of their marriage as a "creative partnership." They do not speak of love. Theirs was a brand, not a marriage, and their life was the ultimate collection.

I catalog the data. He is the kinetic force, the one who gestures, who interrupts, who steers the narrative with a restless, predatory charm. She is the still center, the beautiful object he orbits, her power absolute in its passivity. Her quotes are few; her answers serene and opaque. The hunger, I conclude, is a power struggle disguised as a ménage à trois. He wants to force a reaction from her, to prove she is still a variable he can manipulate. She wants to prove she is beyond his reach, a fixed and immutable object of art. My role is not to be a lover. It is to be a fulcrum.

I choose my armor accordingly. A simple black silk slip dress. Elegant, but pliant. Non-threatening. Its fabric feels like cool water against my skin, a promise of fluidity. My makeup is minimal; my hair severe. I am not there to compete with her beauty, but to reflect it. I am to be a perfect, polished surface against which they can see their own beautiful, fractured faces. I am not going to a hotel suite. I am going to a war, and I am dressing as a neutral territory.

The suite was a study in expensive neutrality. Hushed tones of grey and cream, floors of polished marble that reflected the city lights like a dark still water, so cold I could feel the chill of it through the thin soles of my shoes. The air was scrubbed, conditioned to a perfect, scentless equilibrium, the smell of a space that is perpetually waiting. It was a beautiful, bleached non-place, and for a moment, the sheer lack of personality felt like home.

They were waiting for me, arranged on a white velvet sofa like a photograph of themselves. He was Kenneth, all predatory angles in a black silk shirt, his restless energy barely contained in the taut lines of his jaw. She was Ari, a long, cool drink of water in a slip dress the color of champagne, her beauty a melancholic, passive thing. Her eyes were the blue of frozen lakes. The space between them on the couch was a chasm, a carefully measured distance charged with a silence more profound than the room's.

"Aura," Kenneth said, his voice a practiced baritone that absorbed all the warmth in the room. He didn't stand. "Drink?"

"Of course," I replied, my own voice a smooth, professional glide.

He poured three glasses of champagne, his movements a little too pointed, a little too loud in the quiet room. The pop of the cork was a small, violent report. He was the director, and the performance had already begun. He handed me a glass, his fingers brushing mine in a gesture of ownership he hadn't earned. The crystal flute was arctic cold, the bubbles a fine, aggressive effervescence against my tongue. Ari just watched, her blue eyes holding a profound glacial stillness.

"The script is simple," Kenneth began, pacing in front of the window, his form a restless silhouette against the glittering abyss. "We like to watch. I like to watch my wife enjoy herself. It's been… a while since I've seen her do that."

The words were a stone thrown into the still water between them. Ari didn't flinch. Her gaze drifted to me, assessing. It was not the look of a participant, but of a duelist examining the quality of a weapon she was about to be handed.

"I want you to make love to my wife," Kenneth said, the words blunt, stripped of all romance. "I want you to touch her in all the ways I can't seem to anymore. And I will watch. Every moment."

I turned my gaze to Ari. The blank canvas of Aura's face offered a silent question. Ari gave a slow, languid nod, a queen granting permission for her own execution.

I set my champagne flute down on a marble coaster; the click a tiny, sharp sound of finality. I walked to her, the silk of my dress whispering against my skin. I knelt before her on the thick grey rug. The power dynamic of the room shifted, tipping entirely into my hands. To kneel before a queen is to become her most trusted agent. Kenneth was the director, but I was the one on stage, and I owned the scene.

"Ari," I murmured, my voice a low, intimate hum pitched just for her. I took her hand. Her skin was cool, as if she were sculpted from the same marble as the floor, her fingers long and inert. I brought her hand to my lips and kissed her knuckles, my eyes holding hers. I was performing for an audience of one, and it wasn't the man whose breathing had become a ragged, audible presence by the window.

A flicker. A tiny, almost imperceptible tremor in the ice of her gaze. I had her attention.

I moved slowly, deliberately. I was not seducing a woman; I was restoring a piece of art. My hands slid up her arms, over the cool, frictionless silk of her dress, to her shoulders. I leaned in, my mouth close to her ear, the scent of her perfume a cold, green floral, like crushed hyacinth stems and gin. "He's not here," I whispered, the words a strategic lie. "There is no one in this room but you and me."

It was the most profound lie I had ever told. His presence was a scream in the quiet. His ragged breathing, the faint clink of his glass as he shifted his weight, the sheer force of his desperate, wanting gaze… it was the entire context of the encounter. I could feel it on my own skin, a phantom heat.

My lips brushed the long, elegant line of her neck. I felt a shudder pass through her, a signal of life from the beautiful statue. My hands moved to the thin straps of her dress, sliding them from her shoulders. The champagne-colored silk pooled in her lap, a liquid sigh of fabric. She was exquisite, her body long and pale, her breasts small and perfect. She was a goddess of boredom.

My mouth found hers. Her lips were cold, unresponsive. I did not force the kiss. I simply waited, a gentle pressure, an offering. I felt Kenneth take a step closer, a predator drawn to a stillness he mistook for surrender. And that, I realized, was the key.

I pulled back slightly, my lips still brushing hers. "He wants to see you break," I whispered against her mouth. "Let's give him a performance he will never forget."

Something ignited in the blue frost of her eyes. A cold, beautiful fire. Her mouth opened against mine, and she kissed me back, a kiss of cool, calculated fury. Her hand came up to tangle in my hair, her nails scraping my scalp, pulling me closer. The transaction had been renegotiated. She was no longer the weapon. We were collaborators.

I laid her back against the velvet cushions, my body covering hers. My hands began their work, a slow, meticulous cartography of her skin. My mind, my fortress, was a flurry of activity. I observed the subtle shift in her breathing, the hardening of her nipples under my tongue, the involuntary arch of her back as my fingers slid down the pale plane of her stomach. With every touch, I could feel Kenneth's gaze on my skin, a hot, violating weight. I felt a phantom trace of Evelyn's pen across my own collarbone. The Ridge of Sighs. My own map was being superimposed onto hers.

The act was a strange, three-way monstrosity of wanting and watching. I was the bridge between them, a conduit for a current of resentment so powerful it was almost erotic. My fingers slid lower, through the damp blonde curls between her legs. She was wet. Not with passion, but with something colder. The slick lubrication of revenge.

I found her clit, small and hard, and began to circle it with my thumb. Her hips began to move in a slow, sinuous rhythm. But her eyes never left her husband's. She watched him watch me bring her to life. A faint, cruel smile played on her lips.

Kenneth made a sound, a low, wounded groan. This was not what he wanted. He had wanted to see her desire, but he was being forced to watch her power.

I lowered my head, my tongue replacing my thumb. She tasted of champagne and rage. I worked on her with a focused, clinical skill, my own body a strange, disconnected machine. I felt nothing but a profound, chilling emptiness, a loneliness so vast it had its own gravity. I was facilitating an act of exquisite intimacy, and I had never felt more alone.

Ari's breath hitched. Her hips rose to meet my mouth, her movements becoming more frantic. I felt her muscles clench, the first tremors of her climax. I looked up. Her eyes were locked on Kenneth, and they were wide with a look of pure, triumphant hatred.

"Watch," she commanded, her voice a ragged gasp.

And as she came apart, a long, shuddering cry torn from her throat, she held her husband's gaze. It was not an orgasm of pleasure. It was a detonation. A final, beautiful act of marital demolition.

When it was over, a dead silence filled the suite. Ari lay back, her body limp, her face a mask of cold satisfaction. Kenneth stood by the window, his back to us, his shoulders slumped. He looked like a man who had just witnessed his own execution.

The transaction was complete.

I rose and dressed in the ruins. The envelope with my fee was on the marble console. The paper felt thick and slick; the money inside it dirty, like a relic from a beautiful, vicious crime. Ari didn't look at me. Kenneth didn't turn around. I let myself out, the heavy door clicking shut behind me, sealing them in their silent glittering tomb.

Walking through the late-night streets, the cool air felt like a baptism. The glamour of the evening had been a thin, cheap veneer over something ugly and broken. I had wanted artifice, and I had been handed a masterpiece of it. But it hadn't healed me. It had only shown me another kind of cage.

I get back to my apartment, and the silence is different. It isn't a tomb. It is just… empty. A beautifully furnished void. I walk through the rooms, the ghost of Ari's cold, triumphant climax clinging to me like a residue. I have just come from a masterpiece of artifice, and my own curated life feels like a cheap imitation.

Klio greets me at the door, a small furry complaint about the lateness of the hour. I perform the ritual. I feed her. I pour fresh water into her bowl. The simple mechanical acts are a brief, welcome respite from the noise in my head.

I scoop her up, seeking the familiar comfort. She settles in my arms, a warm, purring weight. I sit on the edge of my bed, stroking the soft fur of her back. The low vibration of her purr resonates in my own chest, a grounding frequency. Usually, this is enough. The purr is a reminder of a life that is simple and real. But tonight, it is just a small, warm machine in a vast cold darkness. It is not enough to fill this echoing silence.

I look at the cat in my arms, this small, perfect creature of appetite and instinct. The only variable. The only thing I allow myself to love without curation. And I am struck by a thought so brutal and so clear it steals my breath. This is the only conversation I am capable of having. A silent communion with a creature who cannot challenge me, who cannot see through my performance, who cannot ask me a single difficult question. My affection for her is just another form of control, another beautiful, living object in my collection.

A wave of loneliness so profound it is a physical nausea washes over me, a vertigo of the soul. The purr is not enough. The warmth is not enough. It is a closed system, and I am suffocating inside it. The old reflex kicks in, a muscle memory of survival forged in the ruins of a dead girl's life: control. A transaction. The work. The work will recalibrate the system. The work will make me breathe again.

I gently set Klio down. She gives me an indifferent blink and begins to wash a paw, already forgetting me. My movements are efficient, a frantic return to a known procedure. I retrieve my work phone from my satchel, the cool, anonymous weight of it a familiar comfort in my hand. My thumb unlocks the screen, opening the encrypted app where the hungers wait, neatly cataloged, their desperate poetry reduced to a clinical queue.

I need a palate cleanser. Something simple. Something that requires nothing but the body as an object. I scroll past the complex requests, the intellectual games, the emotional excavations. I need a lock, not a key. My finger pauses on a new request from a client I have vetted but not yet met. The Horologist. The fantasy is a haiku of beautiful detachment: He wants me to lie naked and motionless on a table for one hour while he uses a vintage stethoscope to listen to my heartbeat. He wants to appreciate the perfect, predictable mechanics of the human machine. He wants a body without a person in it.

It is the perfect Aura gig. A return to first principles.

My thumb hovers over the "Accept" button. I can be there in forty-five minutes. I can wrap myself in the cool armor of the performance. I can become the beautiful, silent machine he wants. I can forget the cold fire in Ari's eyes and the phantom warmth of Arthur's hand. I can forget my own name. The relief of that thought is a siren's song. Just press the button. Disappear.

But I hesitate. The memory of the hotel suite is a sour aftertaste on my tongue. The sheer, ugly emptiness of the performance. The feeling of being a tool in someone else's war. I see myself lying on the Horologist's table, my heart beating its steady, lonely rhythm into the ears of a stranger, and the image warps from one of control to one of profound, terminal isolation.

It wouldn't be a cure. It would be a dose of the very poison that is killing me. The old medicine no longer works. The old escape hatch is just another door into a smaller, colder cage.

The realization is a final, quiet demolition. The last wall of the fortress has just crumbled to dust, leaving me standing in the ruins, utterly exposed, with nowhere left to run. For the first time in a decade, I have no protocol. No thesis. No answer.

My thumb hesitates at Arthur's name, the contact a small, warm ember in the darkness. Too much. Too soon. I cannot face that quiet, disorganized reality. Not yet.

My thumb scrolls up. Through the A's. To the one other name in my phone that is not a client.

Arlo.

I press the button. It rings twice, the sound an absurd intrusion into the late hour. He picks up, his voice, a gravelly, sleep-roughened grunt.

"What?"

I open my mouth, but no words come out. The entire brilliant vocabulary of Aura has deserted me. All that is left is the small and terrified voice of the girl inside.

"Arlo," I whisper, and my own voice is the sound of something breaking. "I think I'm in trouble."

The Bookbinder's Hands

The bell above Arlo's door does not chime. It tolls. A single heavy, final note of brass that announces my arrival, my surrender. I stand on the threshold, a ghost in a black silk blouse, the cold night air clinging to me like a second skin, a slick and miserable film. The warmth of the shop rushes out to meet me, a physical presence, a thermal shock against my chilled face. It is an atmosphere thick with the smell of his life. Paper, a dry and patient scent. Sweet almond glue, a comforting marzipan promise. The sharp, almost bitter tang of leather dye, and the faint, clean perfume of shaved wood. It is the smell of things being made whole, and I am a thing that has just spectacularly and irrevocably broken.

He is at his workbench, a massive slab of scarred maple that has seen a century or more of labor. He does not look up from his work. He is paring the edge of a piece of dark blue leather with a knife that looks like a sliver of the moon, its blade honed to a surgical sharpness. The only sounds are the whisper of the blade across the hide, a sound like a long, satisfied sigh, and the low groan of a late bus shifting gears on the wet street outside.

"You're dripping all over my floor," he grunts.

I look down. I realize it had started to rain in earnest during my walk, no longer a cold, relentless city drizzle. Small dark pools are forming at the toes of my impractical Jimmy Choo heels, the water seeping into the fine Italian leather. My hair, escaping its severe knot, is plastered to my temples in cold, stringy strands. I am a mess. A specimen of complete and utter disarray.

"I'm sorry," I say. My voice is a stranger's, thin and ragged, a frayed thread in the dense quiet of his shop.

He finishes his cut, the motion economical and perfect, a testament to a lifetime of practice. He wipes the blade on a clean cloth and finally looks at me over the top of his spectacles. His eyes, shrewd and kind, do not register surprise. They are the eyes of a man who is rarely surprised by the broken things that find their way to his door. They just take me in. The running mascara I didn't know was there until I caught my reflection in the dark glass of the door coming in. The tremor in my hands, a fine, high-frequency vibration I cannot still. The whole sorry, waterlogged picture.

"Trouble, huh," he says. It is not a question. It is a diagnosis.

I walk further into the shop, into the heart of his quiet kingdom. The floorboards creak a welcome under my weight. I pause to run a hand over a stack of unbound pages on a nearby table, the paper thick and creamy under my fingertips. My pages. The raw material of my fortress. The paper has a subtle, thirsty tooth that seems to absorb the moisture from my skin.

"I can't write the next one," I whisper. The confession feels like a betrayal of my entire religion, a heresy spoken aloud in the sacristy. The words hang in the air, heavy and obscene.

He gestures with his chin to a tall wooden stool. "Sit."

I sit. The wood is cool and solid beneath me. He turns back to his bench, picking up a block of amber beeswax and a length of thick linen thread. He begins to wax the thread, pulling it through the block with a slow, rhythmic motion that is both meditative and powerful. The thread gleams with a low, organic luster.

"Who is it this time?" he asks, his voice a low rumble that seems to come from the floorboards themselves.

"A couple," I say, my voice still small. "Famous. It is… a performance."

"They're all performances, kid. That's the gig."

"This is different. It is ugly. And I am the ugliest thing in the room."

He finishes waxing the thread, its surface now stiff yet supple, and sets it down with a quiet finality. He picks up a bone folder, its tip worn smooth and glossy from years of folding and creasing, and turns to face me. He leans against the bench, a mountain of quiet competence, crossing his thick, ink-stained arms.

"So you have a bad night at the office," he says. "You're a pro. You shake it off. You write the damn entry. You get paid."

"It's not that," I say, the frustration making my voice shake, a humiliating lack of control. "It's the book. The project. It's… the words are gone, Arlo. When I try to write it, to curate it, nothing comes out. It's just noise. There's no analysis. No thesis. Just… filth. My mind is a dead engine."

He is silent for a long time, his gaze steady, a weight I can feel on my skin. He is not looking at Aura, the cool professional with the answers. He is looking at the terrified girl who has called him in the middle of the night, a girl who has finally run out of words.

"You're going about it all wrong," he says finally, his voice softening. He pushes himself off the bench. "You're all up here." He taps his temple with a thick, calloused finger. "The work isn't done up there. The work is done here." He holds up his hands. They are a topography of a life spent creating and fixing broken things.

Stained with ink, scarred by blades, calloused from pressure, and beautiful. "Come here."

I hesitate. A chasm of fear and inertia opens at my feet. He just waits, his patience a solid, unmovable object in the room. I slide off the stool and walk to the workbench, the last few feet feeling like a mile. On a small, clean cutting mat lies a stack of my newest pages, already folded into a neat signature. It is the beginning of a new section of my book.

"You want to write the book, you have to understand the book," he says. He picks up a steel awl, its wooden handle dark with the oil of his skin, worn into a perfect, smooth fit for his palm. "The book isn't words. The book is an object. It has a body. It has a spine. And you have to build it before you can fill it."

He places the signature of pages into a small wooden cradle, a scarred vessel designed for this exact purpose. "Hold this. Steady."

I place my hands on either side of the cradle. The paper is cool and smooth, its silence a rebuke. He takes the awl and, with a single, precise push from the center of his palm, pierces the paper, creating the first sewing station. The sound is a quiet, crisp, intimate violation. A wound. A beginning.

"You don't start with the story," he says, his arm moving with fluid power as he pierces the next station. "You start with the structure. You make the holes. You prepare the way for the thread. You give it a path."

He picks up the long waxed thread and a heavy, curved needle, its eye a perfect, polished void. "Now, we bind it. This is the part that matters. This is what holds it all together."

He begins to sew, his large hands moving with a dancer's impossible grace in the small, precise space. The needle plunges into the first hole, pulling the thread through with a soft rasp. He shows me the kettle stitch, the knot that will link this signature to the next, his explanation a low murmur of technical poetry.

"You've been collecting broken things, Cassie," he murmurs, his eyes on the work, his voice a gentle accusation. "And you've been arranging them in a pretty pattern. But that's not a book. That's a scrapbook. A book… a book has a spine. It has integrity. All the pages, they have to hold on to each other."

He pauses, the needle held aloft, a sliver of silver light. "Your turn."

"What?" The word is a panicked squeak.

"Your turn. I'll guide you."

My heart begins to race, a frantic animal in the cage of my ribs. I shake my head, a useless, childish gesture. "I can't. I'll ruin it."

"It's just paper," he says, his voice soft, but with an edge of command I cannot disobey. "It can be fixed. Now, take the needle."

My hand is trembling as I take it, the cool weight of the steel a foreign and terrible responsibility. He moves behind me, his body a warm, solid wall at my back, a gravitational field. I can smell the faint scent of pipe tobacco and paper dust on his worn flannel shirt. He places his large, warm hand over mine, enveloping it completely. His skin is rough, calloused, a landscape of work against the back of my knuckles. My own hand feels small and useless inside his, a fragile, trembling thing.

"Easy," he rumbles, his voice a vibration that runs through his chest into my back, a low, steadying frequency. "Don't think. Just feel the path. The needle knows where to go."

He guides my hand. The needle slides into the hole he has made. The sensation is electric, a frictionless glide, a perfect, neat passage through the waiting paper. We are not having sex. We are not performing intimacy. We are making something. And it is the most erotic, most real thing I have ever done.

He guides me through the next stitch, his hand still covering mine, his body a steadying presence that blocks out the rest of the world. I feel the tension of the thread in my knuckles, the slight resistance of the paper as the needle passes through, the solid weight of his forearm against my own. My breathing deepens, syncing with his without my permission. The frantic noise in my head begins to quiet, replaced by the simple, physical reality of this one task. The needle, the thread, the paper. His hand on mine.

"Pull it tight," he whispers, his breath stirring the damp hair at my temple. "Not too tight, or you'll tear the page. Just enough. So it holds."

I pull. The thread cinches with a faint, satisfying hum, and the pages come together, snug and secure. A small, perfect piece of a whole. A structure. A spine.

He lets go of my hand. I stand there, my fingers still tingling from the pressure of his, the phantom heat of his palm against my skin. I look at the signature, at the neat, strong line of thread I have just sewn.

And then the tears come. Not the panicked, broken sobs from the other night. These are quiet, hot tears of a release so profound it feels like a dam breaking deep inside me. A corporeal earthquake. I am not crying for the ugly couple, or for Arthur's kindness, or for my own hollow life. I am crying because for the first time in years, I hold a needle instead of a pen. I help to build a structure instead of documenting a ruin.

Arlo doesn't touch me. He just stands there, a silent, steady guardian of my collapse. He lets me cry until the last shudder passes through me, a final, cleansing tremor.

When I am done, I feel scoured. Empty, but cleansed. The air in my lungs feels lighter. I wipe my face with the back of my hand, the salt of my own tears a strange, new taste.

"Thank you," I say. The words are small, but they are real. They are the truest thing I have said all night.

He just grunts, turning back to his bench as if nothing has happened. "You're not done," he says, picking up his paring knife again. "You've got a couple hundred more pages to go." He glances at me, and a rare, small smile touches the corner of his mouth, a craftsman's quiet approval. "Better get to work."

I walk out of his shop and back into the rain. The water is no longer a miserable film. It is a clean and simple fact. I do not feel cured. I do not have a plan. But as I walk home, my hands in my pockets, I can still feel the phantom sensation of the needle in my fingertips, a ghostly pressure of purpose. And I can feel the ghost of his hand, warm and steady, holding mine. I am still a collection of broken things. But for the first time, I know what it feels like to have a spine.

CHAPTER 21

The Stud Finders

The air in their house was not the air of a life. It was the air of a life about to happen. It was a thick, particulate atmosphere of potential, a compound scent composed of raw sawdust, the sharp chemical promise of primer, and the clean, earthy perfume of exposed plaster. The air had a gritty texture, a fine dust that coated the back of my throat. It was the smell of a beginning, and it was so foreign to me I felt it in my teeth.

My heels made a hollow, uncertain sound on the plywood sub-floor. There was no marble here to announce my arrival, no plush carpet to swallow my secrets. Just raw timber and the faint blue chalk lines of a future that was not my own, a ghostly architectural sketch on the floor. The sound echoed in the unfinished space, a sharp, artificial report in a room humming with organic possibility.

They met me in what was going to be the kitchen. Ben and Maria. They were a unit, a matched set of comfortable jeans and soft, paint-speckled t-shirts that smelled faintly of turpentine and their own shared sweat. He had a carpenter's easy strength, a solidity in his stance that seemed to root him to the very floor joists. She had an architect's intelligent eyes, constantly scanning, seeing not just the room that was, but the room that would be. They stood close, his arm a casual, proprietary anchor around her waist, and they did not look at me with the fractured hunger of the Triptych couple, but with a shared, conspiratorial glee.

"Aura," Ben said, his grin genuine and immediate, a flash of white in a dust-smudged face. "Welcome to the chaos."

"We hope you're not allergic to dust," Maria added, her eyes sparkling as she wiped a hand on her jeans, leaving a faint white streak. "It's sort of our main design feature right now."

The hunger here was not for dominance or submission. It was for ritual. They had bought this gutted brownstone, this skeleton of a home, and they wanted to fill its bones with their own story before the walls went up. They wanted to make love in every room, to consecrate the space, to build their future on a foundation of deliberate, joyful carnality. I was to be the catalyst. The high priestess of their groundbreaking ceremony.

"The kitchen first," Maria said, her hand finding the back of Ben's neck, her fingers tangling in the hair at his nape. "It's the heart of the home."

She kissed him, a deep, unhurried kiss that was not for my benefit. It was a conversation between the two of them, a silent affirmation of a shared language. I was merely an observer, a tool they had hired for the job. Like a nail gun or a level. I felt a familiar sense of professional detachment settle over me, a welcome and necessary cooling of my own internal systems. This was work.

Ben lifted Maria onto the bare plywood countertop where a sink would one day be. The wood bowed slightly under her weight with a soft groan. He unzipped her jeans, pulling them down her long legs. I watched, my mind already curating the entry. Specimen M:

The Renovators. Hunger: foundational lust. The desire to intertwine the creation of a home with the affirmation of their physical bond.

Then Ben turned to me, his eyes dark with an uncomplicated, cheerful lust. "Your turn," he said, his voice a low, gentle command.

I slipped out of my dress, the black silk a profane interruption in the dusty air, a slash of expensive shadow in the raw afternoon light. I folded it with my usual precision and placed it on a stack of drywall. I was Aura. The blank canvas. But the canvas felt different here. The air was not sterile. The ground beneath my bare feet was not polished. It was rough, textured, real. I felt a splinter of plywood press into the sole of my foot, a small, sharp point of reality that my mind registered with a jolt of surprise.

Ben's hands found my hips, and they were not the soft, manicured hands of the Collector. They were rough and calloused, the skin a landscape of small scars and thickened pads, the hands of a man who builds things. He guided me forward until I stood between Maria's open legs.

"Touch her," Maria whispered, her eyes on her husband's, a silent, permissive command. "Show me."

I placed my hands on Maria's thighs. Her skin was warm, dusted with a fine layer of plaster, and felt intensely alive. Ben's hands were on my ass, pulling me closer against him. I could feel the hard ridge of his cock pressing into the small of my back through the thin material of his jeans. We were a chain. A circuit. A living bridge between their two desires.

My fingers slid upward, through the soft curls of her pubic hair. She was already wet, her heat a humid bloom against my fingertips. My thumb found her clit, and I began to circle it with a slow, steady pressure. She gasped, her head falling back, her neck a long, vulnerable line. Her eyes closed. Ben groaned behind me, a low, guttural sound of approval, his hips beginning a slow grinding rhythm against me.

This was the work. But Arlo's voice was a ghost in the room. *The book has a body. It has a spine.* I looked around the room, at the exposed two-by-fours that framed the walls. The skeleton. The structure. I was inside the book he had described, a book that was still being built.

My own body, that traitor, responded. A slow, deep heat began to build in my belly. It was not a response to the sex as much as to the context. To the sheer, uncurated potential of the room.

Ben pulled me back from Maria, turning me to face him. He kissed me, his mouth tasting of coffee and sawdust. He lifted me, and I wrapped my legs around his waist. He entered me with a single powerful thrust that drove the air from my lungs, his calloused hands gripping my ass, holding me in place. The rough edge of the plywood counter dug into my back. He fucked me with the steady, driving rhythm of a man sinking a nail. And all the while, he watched his wife. Maria's hand was between her own legs now, her fingers moving in time to our rhythm, her face a mask of fierce, focused pleasure.

It was not a performance of revenge, like with the Triptych. It was a performance of shared creation. I was the conduit, the live wire connecting them. His pleasure was for her. Her pleasure was for him. They were building something, and I was just the beautiful, borrowed hammer.

We moved to the living room, a vast space of exposed brick and floor-to-ceiling windows that looked out onto a skeletal garden. Through the glass, the garden was a mess of churned earth and the stubborn green shoots of weeds already reclaiming the soil. The air drifting in from an open window smelled of damp dirt and the promise of rain, a raw, fertile scent that was the absolute antithesis of my own curated life. A canvas drop cloth, stiff with old paint, was our bed. There, we became a tangle of limbs. I was between them, Maria's mouth on my breasts, her tongue a hot, wet rasp against my nipple, Ben's hand between my legs, his fingers finding a rhythm that made my hips buck against the rough fabric. I looked up at the ceiling, at the raw timber beams crisscrossing the space above us. The spine. Strong. Unadorned. Essential.

The final act was set in the master bedroom. It was the rawest room of all, just a frame of pale wood against the darkening sky, the city lights beginning to prick the blue twilight. Ben laid me down on the sub-floor, the rough wood a cartographer's map of grain and knots against my bare back. He knelt between my legs. But Maria came and knelt beside him. She took his cock in her hand, the gesture so casually intimate it was a kind of violence to my curated world, and guided it to my mouth.

I took him, my throat opening, my rhythm slow and deep. His taste was salt and sweat and the faint tang of his own desire. As I sucked him, Maria's fingers slipped inside me from behind, a sudden, shocking intimacy that bypassed all my defenses. I cried out around him, my body arching, caught between them, a circuit of pleasure completed. They were a team, collaborating on my release.

But it was what Maria did next that broke me. She leaned over me, her mouth close to my ear, her breath a warm cloud in the cool air. "He loves it when you do that," she whispered. Then she kissed my temple. It was not a kiss of passion. It was a quiet, profound statement of fact. You are with us. You are part of this. It was a kiss of inclusion. Of gratitude.

In that moment, I was not Aura. I was not a tool. I was a welcome guest in the most intimate room of their lives. A life they were building, stud by stud, right in front of me.

The heat in my belly, the one I had been suppressing, ignited. It was a wildfire. My own orgasm, unbidden and uncurated, tore through me. It was not the hollow, mechanical spasm the Collector had engineered, nor the shattering surrender of the Somatic Detective. It was a deep, shuddering, foundational quake. A response to the sheer overwhelming force of their shared hope.

When it was over, I lay limp on the floor, my body humming, the scent of sex and sawdust thick in the air. They were wrapped around each other a few feet away, whispering, their bodies slick with sweat. They had forgotten me. The tool had been used. The ritual was complete.

I dressed in the quiet, the black silk feeling like a costume from a different life. The envelope of cash was on the stack of drywall where my dress had been. A complete transaction. But as I walked out of their house, out of their future, I felt the splinters from the floorboards still embedded in the soles of my feet, a physical record of the night I could not catalog away.

Back in my apartment, the silence is no longer an accusation. It is a question. I walk to my desk and look at my book. My beautiful, unfinished, perfect book. It is a stunning piece of architecture. But it is a museum. A tomb.

What Ben and Maria have is a blueprint. It is a mess of sawdust and exposed wires and raw, unfinished potential. It is chaotic. It is vulnerable. And in this moment I realize it is the only thing in the world I have ever truly wanted.

The Confessor

The splinters in my feet are a phantom itch for days. I am a haunted house, but the ghost is no longer a dead woman's perfume. It is the scent of sawdust. The echo of a shared laugh in a half-finished room. It is the specter of a life I cannot curate because it has not yet been built. The feeling is so foreign, so unpleasantly close to hope, that I crave a sanitized environment. A palate cleanser. A transaction of pure, disembodied language.

His request is an antique. It arrives as a typed letter on heavy cream stock, the ink slightly blurred. No email, no encrypted text. He wants four hours of my time. He wants me to sit. He wants me to listen. The fee is an apology for the intrusion. It is perfect. A human deposition. A return to the clinical work of observation.

The address was not a glass spire or a pre-war gem. It was a rectory. A grim, respectable stone building attached to a church whose gothic ambitions had been humbled by a century of city soot. The air inside was cool, still, and layered with the scent of beeswax, lemon oil, and something else. A faint, sweet, smoky ghost of incense that clung to the dark wood like a memory. The air had a physical weight, a density that seemed to slow my breathing, and the silence was not an absence but a presence, a thick velvet curtain that muffled the city to a distant, irrelevant hum. It was the smell of institutional sorrow.

He was waiting for me in his study. The room was a cell of profound, masculine quiet. Books on theology and history stood in disciplined rows. The only art was a severe, beautiful wooden crucifix on the wall. He was Father Michael. He was perhaps fifty, with a scholar's soft middle and the kind of face that has been eroded into kindness by a lifetime of listening to the woes of others. His eyes, behind simple wire-rimmed glasses, were intelligent and deeply, deeply tired.

"Aura," he said. His voice was a quiet, resonant thing made for filling silent chapels. It did not echo; the books on the walls drank the sound greedily. "Thank you for coming. Please. Sit."

He gestured to a worn leather armchair. He sat opposite me in its twin. The leather was cracked in a fine, web-like pattern, and it was cool against the backs of my thighs through the thin silk of my dress. There was no desk between us, no barrier to negotiation. There was no offer of a drink. The proceedings had already begun. He did not ask me to undress. The vulnerability he required was of a different, more terrifying order.

"I have chosen you," he began, his long fingers steepled before him, "because of the nature of your profession. You are a paid vessel for secrets. You have no moral or emotional stake in the confessions you hear. Your silence is a commodity, not a sacrament. It is, I imagine, a purer form of absolution than the one I can offer."

The analysis was so precise, so unnervingly accurate, that I felt a prickle of my old professional pride. He understood the work. He had curated my purpose with a scholar's elegance.

"What is it you wish to confess, Father?" I asked. My voice, Aura's voice, sounded like a blasphemy in this quiet holy room, a sharp, secular note in a sacred chord.

He took a slow, deep breath. "I wish to confess the sin of my eyes," he said.

He began to speak. And the story he told was not one of sordid, predictable transgressions. It was a love letter to the world of the flesh, written from the deepest chamber of an exile's heart. He spoke of the unbearable beauty of the mundane things he was forbidden to touch. He described the way the summer sun filtered through the stained glass, illuminating the bare freckled arm of a young woman in the pews, the fine golden hairs catching the light like a halo. He spoke of the sound of a child's uninhibited laugh during a solemn hymn, a pure, bell-like note of joy that he felt as a physical pang in his own chest. He described the smell of rain on the wool coat of a man who came to him for counsel, a man who smelled of a home, a wife, a life.

His descriptions were not lecherous. They were devotional. He was a connoisseur of a feast at which he could not sit. His celibacy had not numbed his senses. It had honed them to a point of excruciating poetic sharpness. He saw more beauty in a woman's wrist, in the curve of her hand resting on a prayer book, than the Collector had seen in my entire naked body. I felt a flush begin to creep up my neck, a hot, shameful tide. This was not a client. This was a masterclass.

I sat there, a professional curator of hungers, and I felt like an amateur. My collection, my sterile catalog of kinks and power plays, felt like a child's scrapbook of cheap curiosities next to the profound, aching tapestry of his longing. He, who had renounced the world, was more deeply engaged with its sensual reality than I, who swam in its deepest waters for a living.

The eroticism in the room was suffocating. It was the eroticism of pure, unslaked want. My own body, that faithless animal, responded. A slow, deep, molten heat began to pool in my belly, a somatic event I could not catalog away. My nipples hardened against the silk of my blouse, the friction a sudden, startling point of data. I was becoming aroused by the sheer heartbreaking force of his humanity.

"But the true sin," he said, his voice dropping to a whisper, his gaze fixed on the crucifix on the wall, "was not a sin of the flesh. It was a sin of the heart."

He told me about a woman. A widow. She had come to him for grief counseling. She was not a siren. She was just a kind, intelligent woman with sadness in her eyes. He had listened to her, week after week. And he had committed the most profound transgression a man in his position could. He had fallen in love with her companionship.

"The sin was not that I wanted to lie with her," he whispered, and a single tear traced a path down his tired cheek. "The sin, the one that will damn me, is that I wanted to have coffee with her. On a Tuesday. I wanted to hear about her day. I wanted her to ask about mine. I wanted to sit with her in a comfortable silence. The sin was not a desire for her body. It was a hunger for her life."

Coffee. On a Tuesday.

The words were more than a concept. They were a physical impact, a precise puncture just below my ribs. My breath hitched, a sharp, involuntary intake of the incense-laden air. The heat in my belly turned to a cold, spreading dread. I could feel Arthur's hand on mine in the coffee shop, a phantom warmth that was suddenly, unbearably real. This priest, this stranger, had just articulated the one hunger in my entire collection that I could not categorize, could not curate, could not control. The simple, devastating hunger for a shared, ordinary life.

He finally looked at me, his eyes clear and full of a terrible, peaceful sorrow. "That is my confession," he said. "I have desired the world. And I have loved a person in it. I am a man, before I am a priest. And I am a failure at being both."

The hour was up. He rose and walked to a small wooden table. He picked up a plain white envelope and placed it on the arm of my chair. The paper was cool and dry against the leather.

"Thank you, Aura," he said. "Thank you for being a space without grace. It is the only place a man like me can speak the truth."

I walked out of the rectory, the envelope a cold, papery weight in my hand. The city was roaring to life in the early evening. The air was thick with the smell of roasting nuts, exhaust fumes, and a few thousand lives being lived. The sensory data was overwhelming, a sudden, violent assault after the chapel-like quiet of his study. I looked at the faces of the people rushing past me. I saw the bare, freckled arm of a girl hailing a cab, the fine hairs catching the streetlight's glow. I heard the laugh of a couple walking hand in hand, a sharp, private explosion of joy. I saw it all. I saw it through his eyes. And it was unbearably beautiful.

I go back to my apartment. The silence is not a comfort. It is a void. I sit at my desk and open my laptop, my fingers poised over the keys.

Specimen N: The Confessor.

I begin to type, my language sterile and academic. I write of sublimated desire and the eroticism of the forbidden. But the words are lies. My entire thesis, the foundation of my book, the core of my carefully constructed life, is a lie.

It's never about the sex.

I was wrong. I was a fool. It is all about the sex. The touch. The flesh. The messy, beautiful, desperate human need to connect. And the things that are not sex: the pillow forts, the quiet dinners, and the coffee on a Tuesday. Those are not the opposite of sex. They are just a different dialect of the same essential language. The language of love.

I close the laptop. My collection is not a catalog of hungers. It is an index of all the different ways a heart can break. And for the first time, I have the terrifying thought that mine is just one more specimen waiting to be named.

CHAPTER 23

The Somatic Detective

After the Confessor, language is a contagion. Words are a virus that has breached my firewall, and his story is a ghost in my machine, a piece of malware that corrupts every file it touches. I require an antidote of absolute silence, a transaction of pure somatic data. My own thoughts have become a liability, a chorus of unwelcome ghosts. I need an encounter that will exist in the body alone, a place where words cannot follow, where analysis is rendered moot by the sheer overwhelming force of the physical. The request is a prayer answered by a silent god. A private studio in a nondescript building in Chelsea. The fantasy: "A sensory evaluation." There will be no names. There will be no words. The hunger is for the thing that exists before language. It is the perfect, bloodless reset.

The studio was not the dark, velvet-lined space I had anticipated. It was the opposite. It was a shock of white, a physical assault of its absence of color. White walls, a white floor that seemed to emit a low hum of its own, a white ceiling, all bathed in a flat, shadowless light from recessed panels above. The light had no source and no warmth; it simply existed, a forensic glare that rendered everything, including my own skin, as mere evidence. The air was cool and smelled faintly of isopropyl alcohol and clean, sterile linen, the scent of a laboratory or a morgue. In the center of the room was a low, wide table, upholstered in white leather that looked as cold and unforgiving as a slab of marble. It was a space designed for observation, for dissection, and I felt a familiar, chilling sense of being a specimen under a microscope.

He was already there, a technician of the flesh. He wore simple white trousers and a white t-shirt, his feet bare on the cool floor, the silence of his presence a statement of intent. He was lean, with an ascetic's quiet intensity and the unnerving stillness of a predator that has no need to rush. He didn't speak. He simply met my eyes and gave a single, slow nod toward the table.

I disrobed with my usual economy of motion, but the act felt different here. In the unforgiving light, there were no shadows to hide in, no flattering angles. My nakedness was not a statement of power or a tool of seduction; it was a clinical fact, a body presented for examination. I folded my clothes into a neat black square on a white stool, a stark interruption in the room's seamless neutrality, a tiny flag from a conquered nation. I lay on my back on the table. The leather was cool and smooth against my skin, its surface a frictionless plane that offered no comfort, no purchase. I was Aura. The professional. I was ready.

He approached with a single object. Its purpose felt therapeutic, a piece of equipment designed for sensory focus over seduction. It was a thick, padded blindfold of black velvet, weighted with what felt like fine sand. He held it out to me, a silent offering. The instruction was clear. I took it, the velvet cool and dense beneath my fingers, the weight of it a surprise, a small, soft bludgeon. I fitted it over my eyes.

The darkness that descended was absolute. It was a physical pressure, a soft, heavy weight that pressed not just on my eyelids but on my orbital bones, a gentle and insistent force pushing me deeper into the prison of my own body. The darkness didn't just block the light; it seemed to absorb sound, to thicken the air, muffling the faint hum of the lights and the sound of my own increasingly shallow breathing. My gaze, my primary tool of analysis, my first and last line of defense, was gone. My fortress had lost its watchtower. Panic, cold and sharp, pricked at the base of my skull.

He did not speak. His hands found my feet.

His touch was not what I expected. It was not the reverent caress of the Collector or the proprietary grip of a dominant. It was diagnostic. His thumbs pressed into the arches of my feet, a firm, rolling pressure that found points of tension I didn't know I had, sending a sharp, electric signal straight up my spine. He was collecting data. My mind, my fortress, scrambled to do its work, to impose order. Specimen O: The Somatic Detective. Hunger: to possess through diagnosis. To map the soul by reading the body's unconscious testimony, its landscape of tells.

The analysis felt hollow. A recitation of old, useless data.

His hands began their excavation, a work of profound and unnerving patience. He was doing more than simply touching me. He was reading me. His fingers traced the faint silvery line of a scar on my knee, a detail I had forgotten existed. I felt a flash of memory, unbidden and unwelcome, the sharp sting of gravel on a summer afternoon, the taste of blood in my mouth. I was seven. He followed the scar's path once, twice. It was a question asked without words.

Who were you before you were this? My breath hitched. This was not in the script.

He was a cartographer of a different sort. Evelyn had named the territories from above, an imperial survey. This man was taking soil samples. His hands moved over me with the slow and methodical grace of a scholar deciphering an ancient text. He found the small, hard knot of muscle in my back that never quite released, the physical anchor of my control. His thumb pressed into it, not to release it, but to acknowledge it, to say, *I see you*. He found the almost imperceptible roughness on the tips of my fingers, a new texture from the waxed thread and the archival paper of Arlo's workshop. He was not exploring Aura, the perfect, curated object. He was discovering the secret history of Cassie's body.

A slow, treacherous heat began to build in my belly. It was not the hot flush of arousal. It was the molten burn of exposure. I was an open book for a blind man, and he was reading my body in braille.

He moved lower, his hand resting on the flat plane of my stomach. The Pale Plains of Silence. My abdominal muscles clenched into a rigid wall. His fingers splayed, a warm, anchoring weight that seemed to hold me to the table, and then one finger dipped into the small hollow of my navel. A place of no erotic significance. A place of pure, childlike vulnerability, the scar of my first connection to another. A sob, thick and hot, rose in my throat. I swallowed it down, the effort a painful contraction. Control. I am in control.

I would take the scene back. I would make this about sex. I arched my back, a silent, practiced offering of my hips. I let a small, inviting moan escape my lips, a sound of pure artifice. My hand reached out, fumbling in the darkness for him, for his cock, for the simple, mechanical lever that would reset the power dynamic and put me back in charge.

He intercepted my wrist. His grip was gentle but absolute, a quiet negation of my entire strategy. He placed my hand back at my side. He was not interested in the performance. He was interested in the truth underneath it. His hand moved between my legs. He did not lunge for my clit or part my labia with invasive haste. His fingers gently parted the wet folds, and he simply rested there, his thumb making a slow, hypnotic circle on the delicate skin of my inner thigh, a territory of pure potential. He was not taking. He was listening. He was waiting for my body to tell its own story.

And my body, that goddamned Judas, betrayed me completely.

The heat in my belly coiled into a knot of unbearable tension. I was so wet, the slickness a testament to my own undoing. His thumb brushed my clit once, a spark on a gas trail, and a tremor wracked my body. His name is Arthur. The thought was a lightning strike, unbidden and absolute. The memory of his hand on my arm in the restaurant, a simple, kind, devastating touch, I could feel it now, under this stranger's touch. The priest's voice, a ghost in the machine. A hunger for her life. The scent of sawdust, a phantom smell filling my lungs. The feel of Arlo's rough, steady hand over mine.

It was too much. A tidal wave hit the already breached fortress walls. I was drowning in sensation, in memory, with no way to see my way out.

My hips began to buck, a frantic, involuntary rhythm. I was chasing an orgasm not for pleasure, but for the white, silent oblivion I knew it would bring. He met my rhythm, his other hand moving to grip my hip, holding me steady against the table. He was an anchor in the storm I had created. And as I moved, as I clawed my way toward the edge, his thumb found my clit again. With a steady, knowing, unbearable pressure. He was holding me to the point. He was not going to let me escape. He was forcing me to feel it. All of it.

The climax was a system crash. A full-body data purge. It was the moment a building implodes, the load-bearing walls giving way in a cloud of dust and noise. My back arched off the table, a silent scream caught in my throat. And as the convulsions took me, one after another, each one a nail in the coffin of my control, a sound was torn from my lungs. A single, ragged, wounded noise that was the sound of a name I no longer knew how to say. It was the sound of my own ghost finally breaking free.

The Bitcoin payment had arrived just as I entered the building. The transaction was complete.

In the ringing silence that followed, I felt his hands at my temples. He gently, slowly, lifted the blindfold.

The light was an unwelcome intrusion. It was a brutal, painful, unforgiving white. I squeezed my eyes shut against it, tears streaming from the corners, a hot, saline flood I could not stop. When I finally managed to blink them open, my vision swimming, the room was empty. He was gone.

I lay there in the sterile, silent, blindingly white room, my body a ruin, the aftershocks of my release still vibrating in my bones. The silence reclaimed the room. But it was a stranger's silence now, stripped of the familiar metallic gleam of control. It was the vast, humming emptiness of a fortress whose watchtower was obliterated, whose gates had been thrown open, whose warden was dead, and whose prisoner was finally, alarmingly, free.

CHAPTER 24

The Revisionist

The hunger was for revisionist history. A sin more common than lust and more pathetic than greed. It was the desire to unsay the word, to unbreak the dish, to take the other path at the fork in the road. It was a hunger for a life that had never been lived, a ghost story told to an audience of one.

His name was Brad, and he met me in the lobby of a restaurant so perfectly calibrated for romance it felt like a stage set. The lighting was a soft, forgiving gold, a wattage of low contrition designed to blur the hard edges of memory. The air smelled of garlic, wine, and expensive apologies, a carefully engineered atmosphere of second chances. He was a man in his late thirties with a handsome, forgettable face and the frantic, overeager energy of someone trying to stop a precious object from falling. He had already failed. The object was in multiple pieces on the floor. He was just paying me to pretend I could put it back together.

"Aura," he said, his handshake too firm, too long, his palm slightly damp with a nervous, boyish sweat. "Thank you for this. It means everything."

"Brad," I replied, my voice the smooth lubricant for the evening's transaction, a polished and congenial surface. "The pleasure is all mine."

We sat. The tablecloth was a heavy, cream-colored linen, its texture a subtle, extravagant friction under my forearms. He had already ordered a bottle of wine. A Sancerre. It sat chilling in a silver bucket, weeping a slow trail of condensation.

"Is this alright?" he asked, his eyes wide with a desperate need for my approval, a supplicant seeking a benediction.

"It's perfect," I said. The wine, when he poured it, was a crisp, acidic lie on my tongue, its clean minerality a stark contrast to the messy, organic grief it was meant to lubricate.

He let out a breath of relief. "Good. That's good. She, uh, Chloe, she always loved Sancerre."

Chloe. The ghost at our table. The subject of tonight's beautiful, pointless forgery. The terms of the session had been laid out in a series of long, rambling emails. Tonight, I was not Aura. I was Chloe 2.0, the director's cut. The version of his ex-wife from their first date but edited for a happier ending.

"You look beautiful," he said, his gaze flicking from my face to a point just over my shoulder, as if he were superimposing another image onto mine. I had followed his instructions precisely. A simple blue dress, the color of a faded summer sky. Hair down, a curtain of anonymity. A single silver bracelet, its delicate chain bearing a heart charm so generic it felt more like a prop than a piece of jewelry. It was the uniform for a memory.

"Thank you," I said, and then, as per the script, "You look very handsome yourself."

He smiled, but it didn't reach his eyes. "I was so nervous that night," he confided, his voice a low, conspiratorial murmur. "I spilled wine on my tie before I even left the apartment."

I laughed, a soft, practiced sound, a musical note calibrated for reassurance. "I'd have never known."

"No," he corrected, his voice gentle but firm, a director giving a line reading. "No, you said, 'A little chaos is good for the soul.' And you laughed. A real laugh. Can you do that?"

The correction was a small, cold stone in my gut. I was not just a performer. I was a puppet. I laughed again, this time with more force, a brighter, more theatrical sound that felt like a foreign object in my throat. His face relaxed. The scene was back on track.

The entire dinner was a minefield of these small revisions. I ordered the sea bass. He told me Chloe had ordered the risotto, a dish she had loved, and would I mind? Our waiter was only just turning from the table, and I signaled him back with a small, discreet lift of my hand, a seamless motion of professional compliance. The change was made. I was being erased, overwritten in real time. I mentioned a film I had recently seen. He informed me that on their first date, Chloe had spoken passionately about her work as a landscape architect. He then gave me a brief, detailed summary of her latest project, a rooftop garden for a tech billionaire.

I sat there and listened, a ghost wearing another ghost's skin, a palimpsest of a woman. I felt a strange, hollow empathy for this Chloe, this woman whose life was being strip-mined for parts to build a better version of my own. He was not honoring her memory. He was desecrating it. He was taking the real, messy, imperfect woman he had loved and lost, and sanding her down into a smooth, compliant fantasy, a beautiful forgery more pleasing than the original. The act was a quiet echo of my own mentor's theft, and the recognition of it was a familiar, bitter taste at the back of my throat.

The sex, I knew, would be the final, brutal edit.

His hotel suite was as anonymous as the restaurant, a non-place of beige and muted gold, the silence broken only by the low, asthmatic hum of the minibar. He put on music, a soft, inoffensive jazz playlist. He poured brandy, the amber liquid a syrupy, sweet anesthetic. He was following a script only he could read. He sat beside me on the couch, the space between us charged with his desperate, manufactured nostalgia.

"This is the part," he whispered, his voice thick with an emotion that was both real and rehearsed. "This is where I leaned in to kiss you. And it was… perfect."

He leaned in. I met his kiss. His mouth was soft, hesitant, tasting faintly of brandy and regret. I performed my part with technical skill. I let my lips part. I brought a hand to the back of his neck, the fine hairs there a soft, surprising texture. But my mind was a thousand miles away. I was thinking of the Somatic Detective, his silent, patient hands discovering the truth of my skin in the dark. I was thinking of Arthur's simple, devastating gift, the small blue book that sat on my nightstand like a quiet accusation. I was thinking of Arlo, his rough hand over mine, teaching me how to build something real.

Brad pulled back, a flicker of disappointment on his face. "More," he breathed. "More passion. That night… it was like you had been waiting for me your whole life."

I kissed him again, this time with a calculated, theatrical fire, a performance of a passion I did not feel. I pushed him back against the cushions, my body covering his. This was the work. But as my hands went to the buttons of his shirt, the small, cool discs of pearl beneath my fingertips, I felt a profound, chilling weariness. He was not just asking for a performance. He was asking me to lie with my body, to create a physical artifact of a moment that had never happened.

We moved to the bedroom. He undressed me with a reverence that was not for me, but for her. His hands traced the curve of my hip. "So beautiful," he murmured to the ghost in the room.

He laid me back on the bed, the high thread count sheets a cool, impersonal whisper against my skin. He moved between my legs. His touch was gentle, attentive. He was a proficient lover. But with every touch, every kiss, came a direction.

"Tell me you've never felt this way before," he whispered, his mouth at my ear, his breath a warm, brandy-scented cloud.

"I've never felt this way before," I recited, my voice a hollow echo in the quiet room.

"Tell me this is the beginning of everything," he urged, his fingers finding my clit, the touch a clinical, goal-oriented pressure.

My body, that dependable machine, responded. I was getting wet. My hips began a slow, involuntary rhythm. But it was a mechanical response. The ghost in the machine. It was the body of Aura, a series of conditioned reflexes, not the living, breathing landscape of Cassie.

He entered me with a slow and deliberate motion. He looked down at me, his eyes unfocused, seeing a face that was not mine. "Chloe," he breathed, and the name was a branding iron, a jolt of system error that made my muscles clench in protest.

He began to move, his rhythm steady, his body a warm, heavy weight. He was fucking a memory. And I was the haunted bed. He was whispering to her, telling her all the things he should have said that night. Promising her a future that had already been turned to ash.

I closed my eyes. I was the curator, the researcher. I should have been cataloging this, the ultimate hunger for a second chance. But I felt nothing. Not arousal. Not disgust. Just a vast, quiet sadness. The sadness of a beautiful, pointless lie.

He was building to his climax, his breathing growing ragged, his thrusts becoming more desperate. He was chasing a ghost, and he was about to catch her. "Say my name," he gasped, his face slick with a sweat that was not passion, but effort. "Say it like you mean it."

I opened my eyes and looked at him. This sad, broken man, trapped in a perfect moment that had never existed. And in his face, I saw the reflection of my own cage. The sterile apartment. The curated life. The beautiful, hollow woman named Aura. We were both revisionists. We were both forgers of ourselves.

His body tensed. His climax was a low, wounded groan, his seed a hot, pointless punctuation mark inside me. He collapsed onto me, spent, whispering her name into my neck, a final, desperate prayer to a god who was not listening.

The transaction was complete. But for the first time, my own body had refused to sign the receipt. There had been no answering orgasm. No polite, professional spasm. My body, a stubborn, silent dissenter, had remained stubbornly, resolutely silent. It had refused to cosign the lie. It was the one part of the story he could not revise.

I extracted myself from under his sleeping form. I showered, the water sluicing away his scent, but not the feeling of his desperate, lonely grief. I dressed in my own uniform, the black silk a familiar, comforting armor. The envelope of cash was on the dresser, its contents feeling impersonal and sterile, the wages of a sin I had not enjoyed.

As I walked to the door, I looked back at him. He was curled on his side, his face peaceful in sleep, finally reunited with the woman he had just invented.

I had given him what he paid for. A perfect memory. But as I walked out into the cool, predawn air, the city washed clean by the coming light; I knew with absolute clarity that I was done with ghosts. You cannot edit your life. You cannot un-say the word, or unbreak the dish. You can only turn the page. You can only live forward. And for the first time, I felt the terrifying, yet exhilarating desire to write a story that had no script at all.

CHAPTER 25

The Escape Artist

is name was Steve, and his loft was a backstage. The air smelled of old velvet, a soft, dusty scent that carried the ghosts of a thousand audiences, of brass polish, a sharp and metallic tang of effort, and the faint electric ozone of a secret waiting to be revealed. It was a dense, almost tangible atmosphere. Silk cloths in jewel tones of sapphire, emerald, and ruby were draped over unseen shapes, their surfaces shimmering with a low, conspiratorial light. A row of gleaming steel rings, each one a perfect, cold circle, hung on one wall like captured halos. It was a space dedicated to the elegant mechanics of deception, and I felt a profound, unnerving kinship with its owner.

He was a man of quiet, precise movements. He had a magician's hands, which is to say they were hands that never seemed to be doing what you were watching them do, their motion a fluid and hypnotic misdirection. His eyes, a pale, intelligent blue, held the calm of a professional who has absolute faith in his own craft. He was not a client to be studied. He was a colleague from a different discipline, a fellow architect of beautiful, necessary lies.

"Aura," he said. His voice was a low, confidential murmur that the heavy drapes seemed to drink from the air. "The stage is set."

He gestured to the center of the room. A single high-backed chair stood there, its dark wood catching the low light in dull, bruised-purple highlights. It was not intended to be an object of comfort. It was a prop, the centerpiece of a meticulous illusion. I felt a familiar, cool confidence settle in my bones, a welcome and necessary recalibration of my own internal mechanisms. I knew this work. This was the art of the beautiful illusion.

"The performance has one rule," he said, his gaze steady, analytical yet without the clinical chill of Julio's lens. "You must not break the tableau. Whatever happens, you are part of the art. You are the still point in the center of the trick. Do you understand?"

"I am always the still point," I said, the words a familiar and comforting creed.

A faint, knowing smile touched his lips, a subtle and unnerving acknowledgment. "So I've heard."

He did not ask me to undress. He asked me to sit. I did so, my posture erect and my hands resting in my lap, the hem of my short black dress a severe line high on my thighs. I was Aura, the perfect component, ready to be assembled into his fantasy, a beautiful, inanimate object.

He approached with rope rather than the leather or steel I was expecting. Thick, soft, crimson rope that coiled in his hands like a sleeping snake, its fibers holding the low light in a way that made it seem to glow from within. He knelt before me. The gesture was one of reverence rather than submission. He was an artist preparing his canvas, his focus absolute.

He began with my wrists, binding them to the arms of the chair. His knots were far from the brutal simple knots of a sadist. They were intricate and beautiful things, a form of calligraphy in three dimensions. A series of loops and turns that were both a restraint and an ornament at once. The rope was soft against my skin, a dry, almost chalky texture, but its grip was absolute, a steady and undeniable pressure.

My mind went to work, a final, desperate act of self preservation. Specimen P: The Illusionist. Hunger: The eroticism of control made manifest through the performance of its release. He creates a perfect, inescapable trap for the sole pleasure of proving he can escape it.

But the analysis was a whisper in a hurricane, a useless string of words against a rising tide of sensation. As he bound my ankles to the chair legs, the ghosts began to arrive. I felt the phantom trace of Evelyn's pen on my collarbone as a strand of rope brushed against it. The Ridge of Sighs. I felt the memory of the Somatic Detective's fingers, reading the small, forgotten scars on my arms, as the rope slid over my skin. I felt the warmth of Arthur's hand on my waist, a kindness that was a more profound restraint than any rope. The ropes were not just holding my body. They were pinning me to the map of my own history, each knot a new and terrible landmark.

Steve worked in a focused silence, his breathing a soft, steady rhythm. He wrapped a length of rope around my torso, pinning me to the back of the chair. The pressure on my chest was firm, constricting, a slow and deliberate compression. Each breath became a conscious choice, a small rebellion against the binding. He was not just binding me. He was making me profoundly aware of the body I inhabited, this landscape of memory and nerve.

When he was finished, I was a part of the chair. A living sculpture of surrender, a beautiful, breathing trap. He stood back to admire his work, his head tilted, his artist's eye assessing the lines, the tension, the composition.

"Perfect," he breathed, the word a soft puff of air in the quiet room. "The girl in the trap."

Then the show began. He moved through the room with a fluid, mesmerizing grace. He made coins vanish and reappear with a flick of his wrist, the metal seeming to simply dissolve into light. He turned silk scarves into live doves that fluttered in the rafters, their wings a soft, percussive whisper against the high ceiling. He performed for me, an audience of one, and his skill was breathtaking. It was a performance of impossible freedom, and I was the beautiful, captive thing that gave it meaning. I was the cage from which the birds had flown.

And then came the finale. He approached me, his face serious, stripped of its performer's charm. He held up a single ornate brass key. It was heavy, intricate, a small, perfect piece of mechanical poetry.

"Every trap," he whispered, his voice a hypnotic current, "must have a key. It is the promise. The art is not in the lock. It is in the escape."

He did not place the key in my hand. He knelt, and with a touch as light as a moth's wing, his fingers brushed the inside of my thigh, a brief, electric shock against my skin. He slipped the key between my bound thighs. The cold, smooth metal rested against the wet silk of my panties, a shocking point of intimate, galvanic contact. It was an intimate, shocking violation that was not a violation at all. It was a choice. My body responded instantly. A jolt of unadulterated heat shot through me, a low, deep, and immediate pulse of arousal. My clit, already hard with the tension of the scene, throbbed against the unyielding brass.

He stood up and walked to a large wooden trunk a few feet away. It was an antique, bound in dark leather and brass. He opened the lid, stepped inside, and gave me a final, theatrical wink. "The artist must now join his art," he said.

He closed the lid. I heard the sound of heavy locks engaging from within. A series of satisfying, definitive clicks that echoed in the sudden, absolute silence.

The trick was now mine. All I had to do was close my legs, grip the key, and somehow, impossibly, bring it to the locks on my wrists. It was a puzzle. A performance. It was my job. It was the role I had played my entire life.

I shifted in the chair, the ropes biting into my skin, a pleasant, focusing pain. I could feel the key, a cold, hard promise, nestled against my sex. I began to contract my muscles, the small, familiar flex of a body preparing to execute a task, to work it free.

But then I stopped.

The silence in the room was absolute. It was not the cold, sterile silence of my apartment. It was a warm, breathing silence, a silence that was waiting. In the trunk, a man was waiting. Waiting for me to do what I had always done. To find the trick. To solve the puzzle. To escape.

To be Aura.

But what if I did not?

What if I stayed? What if I chose the exquisite vulnerability of the ropes? What if the true escape was not from the trap, but from the relentless, exhausting lifelong need to prove I could pick the lock? What if the true freedom was in the surrender?

I took a breath, a slow, deep inhalation that pressed against my bonds, a conscious expansion into my own confinement. And I made a choice. It was the first choice I had made in a decade that was not a calculation.

I relaxed my thighs.

The key, slick with my own arousal, slipped free. It hit the wooden floor with a small, bright, definitive clatter. The sound was a gunshot. The sound was a final word. The sound was a surrender. It echoed in the quiet room, a tiny, perfect piece of music that was all my own.

A wave of feeling so profound I felt it as it washed through me, a warm and heavy tide. It was not an orgasm, but it was a release. A deep, shuddering, foundational letting go. A quiet, tearless sob of relief escaped my lips, a sound of pure, messy emotion. I had failed the test. I had ruined the trick. I had never felt so free.

A full minute passed. The silence held. Then, I heard the sound of a lock turning, a slow, deliberate click. The lid of the trunk opened, and Steve emerged. He was not smiling. He looked at the key on the floor, its brass form gleaming in the low light. Then he looked at me. He saw the flush on my skin, the dampness in my eyes, the profound, uncurated peace on my face.

He was a master of illusion. He knew a real thing when he saw it.

He walked to me and knelt without speaking. His hands, those clever, deceptive hands, began to untie the knots. His touch was different now. It was not the impersonal touch of a craftsman. It was gentle. Careful. It was the touch of a man handling something precious, something that had chosen not to be broken.

When the last rope fell away, a crimson pool at my feet, I did not move. I just sat there, my body humming with a quiet, unfamiliar energy, the ghost of the ropes still a phantom pressure on my skin. The transaction was complete. But the performance had been real.

After a few moments, I stood and gathered my things. He placed the envelope with his fee on a small table. I retrieved the payment and turned to walk to the door, and then I paused, my hand on the cool brass knob.

"The trick," I said, my voice my own, a little rough, a little unused. "It was a good one."

He looked at me, his magician's eyes seeing right through me, past the performance, past the persona, to the quiet, exhausted woman underneath.

"You were better," he said.

I walked out into the night. The question was no longer what I was running from. It was what I was walking toward. The escape was over. The journey had just begun.

CHAPTER 26

The Stranger

The hunger was for a void. A clean, dark, silent space where I could be a body and nothing more. After the pathetic forgery of the Revisionist, I craved an encounter stripped of memory, of language, of identity itself. I needed a transaction of pure, untraceable sensation. A factory reset for the soul. The request was a balm of beautiful simplicity. A suite at the Gramercy. The room would be blacked out. There would be no words. He would be a stranger. I would be a shape in the dark. It was the perfect bloodless antidote.

I entered the room and closed the heavy door behind me. The click of the latch was a definitive, metallic sound that was immediately swallowed by the atmosphere. The darkness that descended was absolute, a tactile presence, a weight of crushed velvet against my skin and in my lungs. The silence was just as dense, a medium so thick it seemed to press against my eardrums. It absorbed the sound of my own breathing, forcing me into a state of acute and immediate interiority. This was my territory. I was a nocturnal predator, my other senses sharpening to a razor's acuity in the absence of sight. I undressed with a fluid, silent confidence, my clothes a whisper of silk against the quiet air, the friction of the fabric against my skin a known and predictable data point. I folded them on a chair I found by touch, a neat, invisible square of order in the sensory void. I slipped between sheets that felt like cool, still water, my body a blade at rest, poised and waiting in the center of the vast bed.

He was already there. I had not heard him. I only knew by the faint, clean aroma of unscented soap, a smell of pure, unadorned skin, and the subtle warmth radiating from the other side of the mattress, a thermal signature in the cool landscape of the bed. We lay there for a full minute, two ghosts in a machine, the space between us a universe of unspoken rules, a charged and humming emptiness.

Then, his hand found my hip.

It was not a tentative touch, nor an aggressive one. It was a statement of fact. I am here. His palm was broad, the skin slightly rough, a map of a life lived outside of suites like this one. It was a cartography I could feel but not see. My mind, that faithful engine, sputtered to life. *Specimen Q: The Stranger. Hunger: a regression to a pre-verbal state of pure physical communion.* The analysis felt like a child reciting multiplication tables in a cathedral. It was a useless, profane noise in the sacred quiet.

His hand began to move, a slow, patient exploration across the plane of my stomach. And it was immediately, profoundly different. This was not the Somatic Detective's forensic touch, searching for the scars of my history. This touch had no interest in the past. It was a conversation conducted in the absolute present tense. His fingers traced the sharp crest of my hipbone, then dipped into the soft valley of my waist. He was not reading me. He was asking my body a silent question. What do you want, right now?

I would not let it answer. I was the one who asked the questions.

I turned toward him, my movement a deliberate, fluid maneuver to seize control. This was my scene. My hand found his cock, thick and hard, a simple, beautiful mechanism I understood. I wrapped my fingers around him, the skin hot and velvety, and worked my thumb against the sensitive ridge on the underside of the shaft, just below the head. My rhythm was professional and practiced, a metronome of learned skill. I would lead. I would perform. I would bring him to an ordered, efficient release, and I would walk away whole. That was the work.

He did not resist. But neither did he submit. As I stroked him, his hand moved between my legs. His palm settled over my mound, a warm, proprietary weight that was a claim without a question. His fingers didn't flutter or probe; they slid down with unnerving confidence, tracing the seam where my thighs met. Two of them found the slick, swollen entrance to my folds and pressed. Not inside me, but a firm, knowing pressure against the very threshold. I could not call it a caress; it was a statement. A low, deep vibration started in my pelvis, a hum of pure, involuntary response. He was demonstrating his fluency in a language my body could not help but answer. Stimulus: sustained, non-demanding pressure. Response: catastrophic system failure.

My body, that goddamn Judas, responded. The heat was no longer a tide; it was a bloom, a slow, deep molten core that radiated from my pelvis, up my spine, a silent, feverish flush across my skin. I was slick, incredibly so, my wetness a shameless confession against the back of his hand. A confession of what? Of need. Of a truth that had no words. His hand, which had been so patient, went still for a single charged heartbeat. A pause. A recognition.

He shifted, his weight settling over me, the mattress groaning a soft protest in the dark. I felt the blunt, wet heat of him press against me, a question asked without language. And then he entered me with a single, slow, inexorable slide. It was a feeling of being filled, a deep, stretching pressure that bypassed every intellectual defense I had ever built. My inner muscles, those involuntary conspirators, clenched around him in a desperate, welcoming grip. He was still inside me, a hot, solid anchor in the darkness, and for the first time in three years, my mind was blessedly, alarmingly silent. The curator was gone. The researcher had left the lab. There was only the feeling. This feeling.

He filled me. And in the absolute darkness, with no face to study, no voice to analyze, all I had was the overwhelming reality of him inside me. He began to move, a deep, unhurried rhythm that was not a performance. It was a conversation. With every slow, deliberate thrust, he seemed to ask the same silent question. Are you here? Are you with me?

I moved against him, my hips lifting to meet his. I tried to make it a performance. I tried to be Aura, the expert, the one who could ride a man to ruin with calculated precision. But he would not let me. When my rhythm became too practiced, he would slow, his hands gripping my hips, a quiet, physical negation of my professional expertise, forcing me back into the simple truth of the moment. We were just two bodies in the dark, moving together.

The heat was building. The pressure behind my eyes. The knot in my belly pulling tighter and tighter. I was close. Too close. I was losing the observational distance I needed. I was not curating this moment. I was in it. Drowning in it.

He must have felt the shift, the frantic edge to my movements. He pulled out of me. A gasp of protest escaped my lips, a sound I had not authorized. He moved, and then his mouth was on me. Hot, wet, and knowing. His tongue was not the frantic, goal-oriented instrument of a lesser lover. It was patient. It was a question. It found my clit, and it did not attack. It circled. It teased. It paid devotion.

And that is what broke me. The sheer, uncurated generosity of the act. A sob built in my throat. The ghosts were all there, summoned by this stranger's touch. Arthur's kindness. Arlo's steady hand. The Confessor's heartbreaking desire for a simple, shared life. They were not memories. They were living currents, and they were all converging in this dark room, in this stranger's mouth. He was not just making me cum. He was making me whole.

The orgasm was an arrival. It was a tectonic event, a deep quake that started in my womb and radiated through every inch of my body. It was not a shattering, but a fusion. My back arched off the bed. My hands fisted in the sheets. And a sound was torn from my throat, a sound I had never made before. It was not a moan. It was a word. A plea. A prayer forged in a part of my soul I had long ago bricked over.

"Please."

He moved back up my body, entering me again as the last waves of my climax still shuddered through me. He began to move faster now, his own control breaking. I wrapped my legs around him, pulling him deeper, my body no longer a tool but a participant, a greedy, wanting thing. I was not Aura. I was not even Cassie. I was just a woman in the dark, finally, finally wanting.

His release was a low, guttural groan against my neck, his body a heavy, shuddering weight.

We lay there, tangled in the ruins, our breathing loud in the sudden silence. Then, a sound. A sharp, electronic buzz from the nightstand. A phone. Its screen flared to life, a stark blue-white rectangle that illuminated the room for a single, shocking second, a clinical, forensic flash.

In that flash, I saw him. A man. Just a man, handsome in a kind, unremarkable way, his face slick with sweat, his eyes wide with a surprise that mirrored my own. And he saw me. Not the curated mask of Aura. Not the beautiful blank. He saw the wreckage of the fortress. He saw my face, undone and wrecked with pleasure, my hair a wild tangle, my eyes full of a terrifying, brilliant light. He saw Cassie.

The screen went dark.

He withdrew from me, and in the renewed blackness, I felt him rise from the bed. The door opened, a brief, violent slash of hallway light, and then it closed. He was gone.

I lay in the dark, my heart racing, the ghost of the light still seared onto my retinas. I had gone into that room seeking a void, an erasure of self. But I had found the opposite. In the perfect anonymity of the dark, I had been, for the first time, irrevocably, undeniably, myself.

And somebody saw me.

I walked out of the hotel into a city that was no longer a specimen or a threat. It was just a city. The pre-dawn air was cool and tasted of damp pavement and the faint, yeasty smell of a bakery starting its day somewhere nearby. A street sweeper moved slowly down the block, its brushes whispering, washing the grime from the night away. It was a city waking up, and for the first time, I felt like I might be waking up with it.

CHAPTER 27

The Thesis

The hunger was for a footnote. A validation. A single perfect, living data point that would prove a theory he had only ever explored in the sterile quiet of books. It was the most achingly familiar hunger in my entire collection, a perfect and tragic echo of my own past. It was the hunger of a brilliant mind terrified of its own body. It was the hunger that had drawn the blueprint for my cage.

His name was Stuart, and his apartment was not just a memory of my past; it was a haunting. A fourth-floor walkup in a crumbling brownstone near the university, a building that still held the ghosts of my own frantic, ambitious footsteps. The moment I stepped inside, the atmosphere was a physical assault of recognition. It smelled of cheap, bitter coffee brewing into a tarry sludge, of old paper slowly surrendering its acids to the air, and of the frantic, electric hum of an overtaxed mind. It was the specific scent of intellectual desperation, and it was so familiar it felt like I had come home to a place I had burned to the ground. Books were not on shelves. They were in precarious, load-bearing columns that seemed to defy gravity, their spines a mosaic of critical theory and dead philosophy. Post-it notes, hundreds of them in a violent, cheerful yellow, bloomed like a peculiar fungus on every available surface, each one a tiny, desperate anchor for a fleeting thought. It was the den of a young man who had mistaken knowledge for wisdom, a mistake I knew with the intimacy of a scar.

He was twenty-four, maybe twenty-five, all sharp, birdlike intelligence and the kind of profound, painful awkwardness that comes from spending more time with the dead than with the living. He wore a rumpled Oxford shirt, the fabric a soft, apologetic blue, and his glasses were smudged with a fingerprint, a tiny, greasy mark of imperfection that was somehow the most human thing about him. He could not quite meet my eyes. His gaze skittered around my face, landing on my ear, my chin, the wall behind me, as if direct eye contact were a physical blow he was not prepared to withstand.

"Aura," he said, his voice a nervous rush of air, the words tumbling out too quickly. "Thank you. For agreeing to the parameters. I've, uh, prepared a brief."

He handed me two pages of neatly typed, double-spaced text. The paper was still warm from the printer, a faint, clean smell of hot toner rising from it. I took it, my fingers registering the absurd formality of the gesture. It was a thesis statement. An abstract for the evening's experiment. It was titled, "A Performative Exploration of the Hegelian Dialectic in a BDSM Context." It cited Foucault, Butler, and, in a move of such breathtaking academic hubris it was almost charming, Adorno. It outlined a proposed session in which he would assume the traditionally dominant role, and I the submissive, but, and this was the crucial point, we would deconstruct these roles through a continuous verbal analysis during the act itself. He wanted to fuck and take notes. He was terrified. I was home.

I felt the familiar heavy mask of Aura click into place. It was a welcome weight, a piece of armor I knew how to wear. The character of the cool, unreadable professional settled over me like a shroud. "I understand the thesis, Stuart," I said. My voice was the instrument he had paid for, cool, professional, with a hint of indulgent amusement that would put him at ease by affirming his intellectual superiority. "It's a fascinating theoretical framework. Where would you like to begin the experiment?"

He took a deep, shuddering breath, a man steeling himself to leap from a great height. "The bedroom," he said, his voice gaining a sliver of confidence now that we were on the solid ground of his proposal. "I propose we begin with a simple act of... observation."

The bedroom was a more intimate expression of the same intellectual chaos. A mattress on the floor was surrounded by a defensive moat of books, their open pages like the wings of sleeping birds. A single lamp with a bare bulb cast a stark, interrogative light, carving the room into a study of harsh shadows and pale, exposed surfaces. It was the room of a monk, if a monk's god was post-structuralism. He asked me to undress. I did so with my usual fluid grace, a performance of effortless confidence designed to be its own form of control. The whisper of the silk as it slid from my skin was the only sound in the room. I folded my clothes into a neat black square on a stack of literary journals, a gesture of order in his beautiful, frantic mess. I was the perfect specimen. I lay on the bed, my body a blank page for his research, my skin prickling slightly in the cool, book-dry air.

He remained fully clothed, standing a few feet away, a notebook and pen clutched in his hand like a talisman. His knuckles were white. "Observation," he began, his voice shaky, a tremor of nerves belying the academic certainty of his words, "is the first act of possession. By cataloging the subject, the observer establishes the primary power dynamic." He looked at me, his eyes finally focusing, a flicker of something other than pure theory in their depths. Awe. Terror. "Your skin is... pale. The, uh, chiaroscuro effect from the single lamp is pronounced. The line of your hip creates a very distinct S curve, a classic odalisque form."

I lay there, a living sculpture, and I watched him. And as I watched, the ghosts of my own past began to fill the room. I saw myself at his age, in a carrel in the library, my own notebooks filled with a similar desperate, brilliant jargon, my own body a forgotten and inconvenient piece of luggage I had to drag around. I saw this brilliant, terrified boy using the language I had once revered, the language of the curator, to build a wall between himself and the terrifying, beautiful reality of a naked woman on his bed. I saw my own ghost, the ghost of the girl who thought she could analyze her way out of having to feel.

And in that moment, the entire project of my life, the entire thesis of my book, revealed itself to be what it always was: a tragic, beautiful, and utterly pointless fraud. The book was not an analysis of others. It was the blueprint of my own prison, a meticulously researched and elegantly written suicide note for a soul.

"Stop," I said.

The word was quiet, but it landed in the room with the force of a physical blow. It was not Aura's voice. It was mine. Stuart froze, his pen hovering over the page, a droplet of black ink forming at the nib, threatening to fall and stain the paper. "Did I... deviate from the parameters? Was the terminology incorrect?"

"No," I said, and I sat up. The cheap cotton sheet, which smelled faintly of him, of laundry detergent and lonely sleep, pooled around my waist. In that single movement, the tableau was broken. I was no longer a specimen. I was just a woman. "You're executing them perfectly. But the thesis is flawed."

"Flawed? How?" The question was a genuine cry of intellectual panic. His entire world was built on the integrity of a sound thesis.

"Because you're not here, Stuart." My gaze swept the room, at the towers of Foucault, at the frantic yellow notes, at his terrified, intelligent face. "None of this is here." My hand, of its own accord, pressed flat against my chest, over the frantic, trapped bird of my heart. "This is here. This is the only thing in the room that's real."

I swung my legs off the bed. The floor was cool and a little gritty under my bare feet. I stood and walked toward him. He took an involuntary step back, a physical retreat from my un-theorized reality, his back bumping into a stack of books that swayed precariously. He was a startled animal, and I was a creature he had not classified. I was breaking every rule. I was no longer the mirror. I was the thing being reflected.

"Your theory is beautiful," I said, and my voice was softer now, stripped of Aura's professional lacquer, the hard edges sanded away into something gentler, something kinder. "It's a magnificent piece of architecture. But it's an escape. I know, because I built a fortress out of the same materials. The real experiment isn't about watching from the tower. It's about touching."

I stopped in front of him, close enough to feel the nervous heat radiating from his body, to smell the faint, acidic scent of his anxiety. I reached out and gently took the notebook from his hand. The plastic was slick and a little damp from his sweat. I placed it on a stack of textbooks, a quiet, definitive gesture. Then I took his hand. His skin was cold, his fingers trembling, a fine, high-frequency vibration of pure terror.

"Let's try a new thesis," I whispered. The words were not a command. They were an invitation. I brought his cold, trembling hand to my breast. I did not place it there as a prop in a BDSM scene. I placed it there as a question. "The thesis is this: What does this feel like?"

His eyes, wide and dark behind his smudged glasses, were fixed on my face. His breath hitched. I held his hand there, a gentle but firm pressure, letting him feel the warmth of my skin, the soft weight of my flesh, the hard, tight peak of my nipple against the center of his palm, a tiny, explosive point of pure data. I watched his face as a decade of theory dissolved in a single, overwhelming wave of somatic reality. The intellectual framework shattered, and all that was left was the man.

"It's... warm," he breathed. The word was a discovery, a new continent sighted from a great distance. "And... soft."

"Good," I said, a genuine smile touching my lips for the first time. "That's your first data point. Keep going."

I unbuttoned his shirt, my movements slow and deliberate. The small plastic buttons were cool under my fingertips. I was not seducing him in the way Aura would have, with a series of calculated, performative gestures. I was teaching him. And in teaching him, I realized with a jolt that felt like a key turning in a lock deep inside me, I was teaching myself. I pressed his other palm against my other breast, then slid his hands down, over the curve of my waist, the sharp crest of my hip. With every new point of contact, I would whisper the same question, a gentle, insistent mantra. "What does this feel like?"

And he would answer, his voice full of a raw, uncurated wonder, the words simple, elemental, true. "Smooth." "Soft." "Strong." "The curve here... it feels like it was made to fit my hand."

He was not a dominant. I was not a submissive. We were two researchers collaborating on a new and terrifying field of study, and the laboratory was my skin. I led him to the bed and pushed him down gently onto the mattress. The springs groaned a soft, metallic protest. I straddled his lap, his jeans a rough, welcome friction against my wet folds. I looked down at him, at this boy who was a perfect, heartbreaking mirror of my own past, and I felt a wave of feeling so profound it had no name. It was not pity, nor was it lust. It was a fierce, protective, and deeply erotic form of recognition.

"My turn to observe," I whispered. I reached up and gently took off his glasses, folding them and placing them on the floor. Without them, his eyes were softer, more vulnerable. More present. I leaned down and kissed him. It was not a performative kiss. It was a lesson. It was slow, and deep, and it was the truest thing I had done in ten years. His lips were surprisingly soft, hesitant at first, then opening under mine with a silent, shuddering sigh of surrender. He tasted of coffee and fear and a deep, intellectual loneliness I knew like the back of my own hand.

I made love to him with the patient, focused attention of a master craftsman teaching an apprentice. I taught him the texture of my skin against his tongue, the specific, salty taste of my desire. I taught him the changing rhythm of my breathing, the way a touch on the inside of my thigh could make my back arch. I taught him the geography of a woman's body, not as a theoretical map, but as a living, breathing landscape. And in teaching him, I was learning myself. For the first time, my body was not a tool for a transaction, but an instrument of connection. For the first time, I was not analyzing the sensation from a safe, clinical distance. I was just... feeling it.

He was a feverish and grateful student. His hands, which had been so clumsy and cold, learned the language of my body with a startling speed, their touch growing warmer, more confident. His mouth, which had only spouted theory, learned how to worship, his tongue tracing the line of my collarbone, the curve of my breast, with a reverence that felt like a form of prayer.

He entered me as an explorer entering a new world, his eyes locked on mine. And as he moved inside me, I met his gaze. There was no fear left in his eyes. Only a brilliant, shining, disorganized presence. He was here. And so was I.

The orgasm, when it came, was not a demolition. It was not a surrender. It was a quiet, profound, and deeply peaceful arrival. It was not the shattering, soul-stripping event of the Somatic Detective, or the hollow, mechanical spasm of the Collector. It was a wave of pure, warm light that did not break me, but fused me back together. It was the first orgasm of my new life. It was the first orgasm that belonged to Cassie.

We lay there afterward, tangled in the cheap sheets, the air thick with the scent of sex and the quiet hum of two people who had just discovered a new continent. The single bare bulb overhead seemed to cast a softer, kinder light now. The envelope with my fee was on his desk, a stark white rectangle in the gloom. The transaction was complete. But it was not the transaction he had paid for. It was the one we had both desperately needed.

I dressed in the quiet, my movements no longer the sharp, precise gestures of Aura, but the softer, more human motions of a woman who was tired, and sated, and whole. The black silk felt like a costume I was finally taking off.

As I stood at the door, he spoke. His voice was no longer nervous, but quiet and clear, resonant in the small room.

"Thank you."

I looked back at him. He was just a young man, sitting on the edge of his bed in his rumpled clothes, looking at me with eyes that were finally, truly, seeing.

"You're welcome, Stuart," I said.

I walked out into the cool night air, leaving the envelope where it lay on the desk. I did not feel the smug satisfaction of the curator, or the hollow chill of the performer. I felt... quiet. I felt a peace so deep it was a form of strength.

I go home. I feed Klio, her soft, furry weight against my leg a simple, welcome fact. And I sit at my desk. I look at the beautiful hand-bound book Arlo has made for me. My collection of cages. I open it to the next blank page. My fingers, steady and sure, hover over the keys.

I type the title.

Specimen Z: The Thesis.

The words look like a relic from a dead language. A beautiful, meaningless artifact. I watch the cursor blink for a moment, a tiny, patient heartbeat. Then, with a quiet, definitive series of clicks, I delete it.

I type a new title.

Chapter One: The Student.

I begin to write. But the language is different. It is not sterile. It is not academic. It is warm. It is simple. It is true. It is the first page of a new book. And for the first time, I know, with an absolute and unshakable certainty, that the author is me.

The First Page

Six months later.

The silence in the coffee shop is complex and layered, a stark contrast to the sterile, weaponized vacuum I once engineered. That silence was polished, cold steel, a perfect and intentional absence. This is the opposite, a perfect and intentional presence. It is composed of the low hiss of the espresso machine, a contented mechanical sigh, layered with the clatter of ceramic mugs on wooden saucers. Beneath that is the murmur of conversations I have no interest in cataloging, a soft, textural wash of sound. The final note is the scratch of a student's pen on paper at the next table, a sound of creation, not curation. This is the sound of a world that is beautifully and messily alive, and I am finally just one small part of it.

I take a sip of my latte. The mug is a satisfying weight in my hands, its ceramic surface radiating a steady warmth. The bitterness of the espresso is softened by sweet, creamy milk, the foam a soft cloud on my upper lip. I wear jeans. The denim is a soft, coarse texture against my skin. My sweater, a blend of wool and cashmere the color of a rainy sky, is gentle against my neck and wrists. A simple silver bracelet rests on my wrist. It is not a prop or part of a uniform. It is simply mine. My mousy brown hair is pulled back in a loose, messy knot. A few stray strands curl at my temples. I barely notice the faint, ticklish sensation.

Across the small, scarred wooden table, Arthur is nearing the climax of a story involving a squirrel. His eyes, the kind, tired blue of a faded chambray shirt, are crinkled at the corners with the effort of suppressing his own laughter. He is not a specimen to be analyzed; his gestures are not data points to be logged. He is simply a man I enjoy, a man whose quiet, steady presence has become a kind of harbor in the new, uncharted waters of my life. We meet for coffee. On Tuesdays. It is a ritual so breathtakingly normal it still feels like a radical act.

"…and there he was, perched on the very top of the feeder, this tiny furry Napoleon Bonaparte, just staring at me with those little black bead eyes, as if to say, 'This is my seed now, old man. What are you going to do about it?'" Arthur's hands, which are broad and etched with the fine lines of a life spent turning pages, animate the story, sculpting the villainous squirrel from the coffee-scented air.

"So what did you do?" I ask, leaning forward, the warmth of my own mug a pleasant heat against my chest.

"What could I do? I'm out there in my bathrobe, a man of sixty-eight, shaking my fist at a rodent. My new neighbor, the one with the prize-winning roses, just stares at me over the fence with this look of profound pity. And all I could think was, 'This is it. This is how I've finally, completely, lost my mind.' I surrendered. I went back inside and made toast."

A laugh escapes me. It is not Aura's practiced, musical trill, a sound engineered for charm and dissimulation. It is Cassie's laugh, and it feels like a rusty hinge being forced open. It is a little uneven, a little loud, a clumsy and genuine eruption of sound that feels both foreign and deeply familiar in my throat. The physical sensation of it, the contraction of my diaphragm, the way it makes my eyes water just slightly, is a small, startling miracle.

"You should have charged him rent," I say. The joke is easy, unstudied. It rises and leaves my mouth without passing through the rigorous, multistage vetting process of my old internal monologue. "Or at least demanded a portion of his winter stores as tribute."

Arthur's smile is the reward. It is a genuine, uncurated thing that transforms his face, erasing some of the tired lines around his eyes and replacing them with a gentle, brilliant light. The warmth of that smile is no longer a terrifying, invasive force. It is just… warm. A small, clean fire in the middle of a Tuesday afternoon.

My gaze drifts for a moment, past his shoulder, through the large plate-glass window of the shop to the ceaseless, messy hum of the city street. A woman in a red coat hails a cab, her arm a slash of brilliant color against the grey afternoon. A bicycle messenger weaves through the traffic with a fluid, suicidal grace. Each person is a story, a collection of hungers and histories I have no need to dissect. They are simply part of the living texture of the world. And in that moment, my mind drifts to the book. The Client Book. It sits on a shelf in my apartment, a quiet, dark rectangle of a thing, nestled between a worn paperback history of Venetian art and a slim volume of poetry I have not yet read. Bound in the dark, oil-tanned leather Arlo chose, its pages filled with my own cold, precise script. A closed volume. A finished work.

I feel no hot shame when I think of it, nor do I feel the cool, smug satisfaction of a thesis proven. It is simply a history. An artifact from an archeological dig into a life that is no longer mine. It is a meticulous, beautiful, and heartbreakingly honest account of a woman who was a masterful curator of every cage but her own. A woman who was so terrified of being a specimen that she built her own vivarium and called it a fortress. A woman I used to be. The memory of her, of Aura, is not a ghost that haunts me, but a photograph of a stranger I once knew intimately, a stranger whose choices I can finally begin to understand with a quiet, dispassionate compassion.

The silence that has fallen between us is a new element in my taxonomy of quiet. It is not the stretching, performative silence I once wielded with clients, a void designed to compel confession. It is not a weapon. It is a space. A comfortable, breathing room built for two. It is a silence that does not need to be filled.

"You're a thousand miles away," Arthur says gently, his voice a quiet invitation, not an accusation, pulling me back from the window, from the past.

"Sorry," I say, my focus returning to his face, to the kind, patient intelligence in his eyes. "Just... thinking about a project I finally finished."

"Ah, the big art history book?" he asks, remembering a detail from one of our earlier conversations, a piece of the elaborate, professional fiction I had constructed for him, for everyone.

I consider the lie. The old, easy deflection. *Yes, the research was exhaustive.* The words form in my mind, a familiar, well-worn path. But they feel like a foreign language now, a dialect I no longer have any use for. The truth, or at least a shard of it, feels simpler. It feels lighter.

"Something like that," I say. And it is, I realize, the most honest answer I could possibly give.

He doesn't press. That is the quiet miracle of him. He never does. He accepts the spaces I leave, the questions I do not answer, with a gentle, unassuming grace. Instead, he reaches across the table. His hand, warm and smelling faintly of pastries and the lemon soap he uses, covers mine where it rests beside my mug. His touch is not a question or a claim. It is not a diagnostic tool or a prelude to a transaction. It is an anchor. His skin is warm and dry, the palm slightly rough, the hand of a man who has held books, his wife's hand, and a coffee cup for a long and decent life.

In my mind, a ghost of a line I wrote a lifetime ago echoes, the thesis statement of a book and a woman now closed to me. *What I am actually selling is a finely crafted mirror.* The words feel like a beautiful, sad artifact from a forgotten civilization. For years, I was a perfect, cold reflection. A curated and flawless surface designed to show others their own desires, their own brokenness, while revealing nothing of my own. I was a magnificent hollow thing.

But Arthur is not looking for a mirror. He is looking at me. His gaze is not a reflection. It is a form of quiet, steady light. And his touch is not a reflection. It is a warmth that sinks past the skin, past the muscle, a gentle and persistent heat that seems to be searching for the bone.

Aura would have analyzed the gesture. She would have cataloged it. Assigned it a meaning within a pre-existing theoretical framework of grief, loneliness, and transference. She would have noted the slight pressure of his thumb on her knuckle as a nonverbal signifier of nascent affection. She would have been brilliant, and she would have felt absolutely nothing.

I just feel it.

The warmth is a simple, undeniable fact. I do not flinch. I do not pull away. I do not even think. My fingers, of their own accord, which for so long were instruments of either analysis or a detached, professional carnality, make a new choice. They curl upward, lacing through his. The gesture is small. Quiet. And it is the most monumental act of my life. His fingers tighten around mine, a silent, answering pressure.

In my bag, next to my wallet and my keys, is a new notebook. It is not the hand-bound leather tomb of my past. It is a simple, elegant thing with a cover the color of a stormy sea. Its pages, a gift from Arlo, are thick, creamy, archival stock. They are also completely, terrifyingly, and gloriously blank. The blankness is no longer an accusation. It is an invitation.

Arthur gives my hand a gentle squeeze. I squeeze back. The simple reciprocal pressure is a new kind of language, a conversation held in nerve and bone. And for the first time, I feel the exquisite and boundless relief of a story that is only just beginning.